DETROIT PUBLIC LIBRARY

BL

DATE DUE

ILL
ILL
FEB 27 1997

THE TRANSGRESSOR

JULIAN GREEN

The Transgressor

TRANSLATED BY ANNE GREEN

PANTHEON

c. 3

Title of French edition
Le Malfaiteur
Librairie Plon, Paris

B.L.

Copyright © 1957 by Pantheon Books, Inc.
333 Sixth Avenue, New York 14, New York
Library of Congress Catalog Card Number: 57-10234
Manufactured in the U.S.A.

0886-11-264

PART ONE

When Hedwige, orphaned dependent of the Vasseurs, fell in love with Gaston, Jean tried to warn her of Gaston's deviation. But his warning came too late to avert tragedy.

UNTIL NIGHT WAS OVER and the birds began chirping in the trees, Jean sat at his table before a blank sheet of paper and an open book whose pages remained unturned. A small lamp shed its placid light over the watcher's hands, long narrow hands that seemed to sleep, like tired workers.

Not a sound throughout the house, but out of the garden came a whispering from the linden where the first autumn breezes loitered. It had rained a few minutes before and a kindly smell of earth stole gradually into the room, like a gust of memories. Whenever Jean felt anxious and breathed in this fragrance as it rose from the innermost depths of the soil, it cheered him to the heart. Perhaps that was why he smiled.

He still looked very young. His unlined face had kept the faintly astonished expression that is seen in children, but his eyes and mouth were those of a man who had suffered: there was something hurt in his glance, something repressed in the shape of his lips, as though too much that should have been said had remained unspoken. If he kept out of harm's way, further curtailed his modest ambitions, and stuck faithfully to his books and garden, he would go quietly to an honorable death. Far better for him to hide and allow life to go past him, like a great resounding stream. Others were cut out for wrestling with life, but his only difficulties were to be spiritual ones, and if he ever hungered, it would be for food that the world cannot provide. All this was so clearly written in his face that a stranger would have had no trouble in deciphering the few signs inscribed there by fate. But was Jean aware of this? One of the singular aspects of our life is that we are ignorant, sometimes to the very end, of what almost anyone might have told us.

The walls behind him offered nothing but their white surface over which his shadow moved at times, nodded its head. In a corner, a big, low bed with blankets tossed back in a heap, and on an old chest of drawers with brass handles, eight or ten books: that was all. The table at which he sat was made of deal, like a kitchen table, and the plum-colored dressing gown wrapped around his long, slim body showed signs of wear and tear, but it was the only garment he liked, the only one in which he did not feel disguised, for its limp, threadbare material was not the homespun of a monk's robe, or the dreary suit we all wear, it was something intermediate: the uniform of a big, capricious, undisciplined army that is scattered over the face of the earth, an army of solitary, gentle anarchists.

The watcher drew the folds of this friendly old rag over his legs and rubbed his knees intently. What could he be thinking about that he sighed so deeply? Did he imagine that insomnia would help him to make up his mind? He picked up a pen and held it in his skillful hand, examined it as though he had never seen it before, and then, without dipping it in ink, ran it over the paper and wrote a few words in invisible letters, conclusive words, perhaps, but words that no one would ever read. And now he threw down the pen and closed his book. He was not angry, he was simply resigned. After which, elbows on the table, he rubbed his head diligently and, wantonly ruffling long, vigorous locks threaded with silver, seemed to whisper something confidential to the wide sleeves above his bare arms.

"All this is ridiculous," he said under his breath.

The air freshened suddenly and the sky grew lighter. In some distant courtyard, a blackbird began a mocking little song, then forgot how the tune went on. Jean then blew out the lamp and could see nothing at first, but as his eyes became accustomed to the darkness, he watched dawn rise behind the black roofs. It rained softly, the bird no longer sang. Jean remembered that when he was a child, the blackbird's song made him laugh with joy as he lay all alone in his bed, and that he would whisper between his fingers, almost imperceptibly, for he knew that he was not to wake his mother: "Do you hear the bird, Mamma, do you hear it?"

There was something so painful about such memories at present that Jean's heart grew a little heavy. For the happiness of childhood had been the only one that he had ever fully enjoyed, and he usually avoided dwelling on it. But that morning, he could not control his memory and it led him where it pleased, artfully marking out the lost path, recalling, with cruel sweetness, the smiling face of a woman, her arms filled with field flowers, still young, tiny, dressed in pale blue gingham, and her eyes were grave, like her son's, but no matter how often he whispered the name he gave her, she did not hear, for he would go to her, but she would not come to him.

If you were here, he thought. If you knew, poor Mother!

What was the good of wishing his mother could return? Would she not be the last person in whom he would confide, the very one to whom one should lie to the bitter end? No. Far better to keep his anxiety to himself, and if the world believed him to be other than he was, it could not be helped. Had he not been forced to keep silent?

A voice answered *no* very distinctly to this question, but Jean knew that answer was coming. To his mind, the world did not care to know. Why tell people what they are determined to ignore? No one asked anything of Jean, he was highly regarded. Yet something in his nature made him wish to destroy his life as one would tear down a patiently built house. He himself could not understand it. He was constantly tempted to tell a truth that was not at all fit to be told. So he took the sheet of white paper that had lain before him for almost an hour, quickly wrote a few lines in a large slanting hand, then stopped, read what he had just written in the uncertain light of dawn, and tore the page up, as he had torn up twenty others.

That is how he spent the early hours, in aimless dreams, in useless efforts to finish the page he had begun. He lacked courage. He preferred not to think about the way in which he had spent the night. He no longer smiled as he had a few minutes before, but bent his head slightly, as though something weighed it down, and nothing could be read in his face at present but sadness and disgust. He thought of what he might have been, of his tragically warped life.

He sometimes wondered what opinion the other inmates of the house had of him. His cousin, Mme Vasseur, whose guest he was since the war,* considered him only in the light of a scholar, as she expressed it with exasperating naïveté. She gave him a small pension, on

* That of 1914.

account of which she considered herself charitable. Not that she liked him much, but she needed the verbal gratitude that he lavished on her and felt agreeably moved every time he conversed with her about her goodness. She sighed a little then and preened herself.

Mme Pauque, the latter's sister, professed to have the same opinion as Mme Vasseur concerning the talents and steadiness of the man she called the hermit of the Rue Valentin. In Jean's eyes, she seemed scarcely more intelligent than her sister and was a silent, courteous woman who always kept in the background when she should; it was impossible to know what went on behind that smooth, placid brow; nothing, probably.

Very rarely, Mme Vasseur's daughter chanced to knock at Jean's door. That happened when she was bored and because it sometimes amused her to disturb a man who never paid her the shadow of a compliment. Under pretense of borrowing a book, Ulrique would wander around him, casting a glance of curiosity and contempt over the bare room. To live in such discomfort and to be so retiring was beyond her, but as she would never have condescended to think over anything that she did not understand, she simply concluded that the old bachelor was mad, and that his madness assumed a rather boring form.

The three women counted for very little in Jean's life and he scarcely cared if they had a false impression of him, or thought him better or worse than he really was, but he was far more anxious that little Hedwige should not misjudge him, for he was fond of the nice little provincial girl, as fond as an awkward, studious man like himself could be of a lively young creature whose frankness sometimes proved indiscreet. Mme Vasseur had taken her in when her parents died, so Hedwige had lived with the family for the past ten years. Her circumstances were much the same as Jean's and that brought them together. What Jean respected in her was a rather absurd candor, which the family considered bad form: Hedwige never lied; neither self-interest nor politeness could persuade her to disguise the truth. For this reason, Mme Vasseur allowed her to meet only tried and trusted friends, although her young relative was pretty and of marriageable age. Jean could have been more intimate with Hedwige, if he had not been so retiring, but she laughed a trifle too much and teased him about his gray hair and staid expression; and then, above all, she credited him with virtues that he did not possess. That in itself was enough to fight shy of her at moments when he felt like confiding in someone.

Next came honest M. Vasseur, who went through life without suspecting evil. He was a smiling, bald little man, and although he never knew it, his wife and daughter Ulrique were mortally ashamed of him. He had managed to grow rich without wronging anyone and his innocent soul showed in a beaming face. There was something so preposterous in the idea of confiding in M. Vasseur, however, that Jean could not help laughing.

And lastly, Raoul, Ulrique's husband. Jean could not bear this frisky ass and took the greatest pains to avoid him. He did not care to know what Raoul would do if he were prime minister, or how he felt about the coming races, or at which towns he intended to stop on the gastronomical tour he and some dozen other gluttons were planning. Jean guessed Raoul's opinion of him, but it left him indifferent. Raoul's brain welcomed only the simplest ideas, and "parasite" was the term that baldly summed up what he thought of Jean. What good would it be to enlighten him? Jean felt equal to reeling off, then and there, all the vindictive platitudes that Raoul would give vent to, if he knew about him.

In the stillness of chilly dawn, it seemed to Jean that these familiar characters filed past him, with their worries, mannerisms, and ridiculous little ways. He pledged himself to the effort of meeting these men and women halfway, to understand them better, and even—who could tell?—to love them. Then, beyond a doubt, they would return his brotherly impulse. . . . Were they not, in themselves, the whole of humanity? Nothing could change them, even though their number were infinitely multiplied. Jean went a step further: he wanted to be one of them, for he felt a sudden horror for the mental solitude in which he lived; he wanted to mix with the innumerable family, whose name is *everyone else,* and be swallowed up by it. Both courage and cowardice would be required to accomplish this, to renounce oneself and take the vows exacted by the multitude: "You shall eat as we do, think as we do, and also *love* as we do. Be like us, or we'll smother you."

Jean shrugged his shoulders. He did not feel like wrestling with everyone. Sooner or later a crushing majority of Vasseurs would break his spirit, and such warfare no longer interested him, for his fits of indignation were short-lived. Better to hide, keep silent, and occasionally filch a little of the happiness that life offers so many. He would be like a very poor man who steals bread from a baker. After all, she could not delay too long in coming, the old nurse who brings tired children home when the day is done and their eyes fill with shadows, and their toys no longer amuse them, the old nurse with a face veiled in black, who watches over us with an all-devouring love.

Chapter 1

FÉLICIE SAT BY THE WINDOW in a chair that resembled a *prie-dieu.* Her feet on the rungs of another chair facing her, the little gray-haired creature mended a tear in a magnificent brown silk petticoat that spread over her knees. She bent double to see more clearly and without interrupting her work, sighed softly from time to time. At last, when she had made the last stitch, she leaned forward and bit off the thread with her teeth, looking as though she were browsing the splendid material.

Now she stood holding at arm's length the much pleated and furbelowed garment. Félicie regarded it with a mixture of loathing and admiration that made her black eyes gleam behind steel-rimmed pince-nez. That petticoat was the image of Madame, Madame and her highfalutin airs, Madame and her disdainful walk, Madame and her luxury; and it smelt nice, like Madame. Chypre (Félicie sniffed) or violet? What Félicie found most difficult to forgive in her employer was not her happiness, an aggressive happiness that had to be accepted as one puts up with bad weather in winter, but her condescending pity for humble folk. Félicie would have infinitely preferred Madame to be arrogant to the bitter end, harsh and beautiful as an unjust queen, without her unaccountable qualms of conscience that found expression in ridiculous gifts accompanied by offensive

DET PUB LIB

remarks. And so, she felt quite certain that she would fall heir to that lordly petticoat, she, a poor old woman who could have no possible use for the glittering rag. And, most painful of all, the grateful words that would rise to her lips from a heart filled with rage. "Madame is too kind! Madame is really *too* kind!" With luck, however, Félicie would succeed in selling the petticoat. But if it was not worn too long, at that. The Jews in the Rue de l'Ecorcherie were so inquisitive about what they bought! They felt for places where the silk might be thin with the tips of their dirty fingers, and how they would snigger when they discovered the tear!

She laid the garment on a chair and fell to scratching her scraggy neck with the pince-nez she held between thumb and forefinger. Short and a little humpbacked, she tried to make the most of her stature by pushing her stomach out and laid her hand on her hip. In this defiant attitude, one she often took when alone, she pursued an angry meditation for a few minutes. She looked the whole world in the face, she braved Madame and the Jews. Although she was well over fifty, the poor woman worked herself up like a little girl and played her favorite role, for her own benefit: she acted the part of the downtrodden rising in revolt. Her worn cheeks flushed and even her gray locks seemed to rebel around a narrow forehead. With the obstinacy of a simple soul, she mentally turned over questions to which there was no answer. Why did others have everything when she had nothing? What freak of fate obliged her to live in a dark garret when Madame had been given a house twenty times too large for her? Why was she forced to wear a patched and shiny serge dress winter and summer, and live on cold cuts because she was too tired to cook herself a meal when she reached her room on the sixth floor in the Rue des Augustins? Why? What fault had she committed to be punished by breaking her back sewing from morning to night? She sometimes felt like crying, more from anger than from sadness and, above all, from weariness. She stood on the threshold of old age without having yet discovered that life was worth living; she only wondered that anybody should cling to it and should dread, as she did, the time when this ferocious jest would end.

She went back to her chair by the window after a few minutes and, crossly picking up a roll of blue material, began turning it over and over. No doubt she would end by going blind sewing on pitch-black stuffs, as she put it, but who cared, she would like to know? Settling her pince-nez on a pugnacious little nose, she tore a needle from her breast. If customers only knew what went on in the minds of those who work for them, all the rage that can be sewn into the stitches of a seam! The old maid smiled as she thought of it, and tackled her work with renewed energy.

The room where Félicie sewed was at the top of the house, next to the servants' rooms. It was a sort of attic that looked out on a quiet little street. A cradle and some outworn toys in a corner showed that a child must have lived there, and the skirting boards below the faded flowered wallpaper were scribbled over in black pencil. In Madame's mother's time (this expression was often on Félicie's lips) the dressmaker often worked in the old baroness' room; the latter was a good, simple soul who had not forgotten her modest birth and knew how to talk to humble folk: concerned over their welfare, wondering whether they were warm enough, even having a joke with them, which made her daughter, the haughty Mme Vasseur, shudder.

The latter made no bones about driving Félicie from the first floor, when the baroness died. First of all, she thought it indecent to have Blanchonnet in the room where her mother had given up the ghost. Blanchonnet was the dummy used by the dressmaker for trying on clothes. Headless, armless, legless, it offered the appearance of an antiquated woman of fashion after a barbarous execution. This showy torso, covered in a black fabric that was shiny over the breast and hips, was raised to a normal height by a tall stand of painted wood, but Félicie was obliged to climb on a chair when she wished to fit a bodice on Blanchonnet. True, she might have unscrewed the dummy and stood it on a chair or table; that she would not do; she dared not, perhaps. A strange fear came over her sometimes when she thought suddenly of Blanchonnet who stood behind her, watching her as she worked silently; or when she arrived in the morning, her mind full of things that had nothing to do with the dummy and she saw its large, motionless outline in front of the window; she gave a start, then, and although she murmured with a smile: "Ah, it's Blanchonnet!" this did not prevent her heart from beating a little faster.

This feeling had grown since the death of the old baroness, for a reason that the dressmaker would not even admit to herself, for, there again, she dared not. The fact was that Blanchonnet had been present at the poor old lady's last moments. The dummy knew all the phases of that swift, commonplace tragedy, for in the panicky confusion of the last few minutes, no one had thought of removing this absurd witness. Overturned bottles, misinterpreted directions, tears and screams, Mme Vasseur's annoyed voice, all this gloomy excitement could have been described to the dressmaker by Blanchonnet, granted a human voice could issue from a cardboard bust. Yet, after a certain fashion, this very silence exalted Blanchonnet in Félicie's eyes. Formerly, she had simply found it useful and like any other dummy. However, since it had been present at a death by apoplexy, it seemed, through some mysterious process, to have come to life. Félicie began to regard it as a traveller who had ventured into forbidden regions and was not to tell what he had seen there. At times, the dummy appeared to be thinking over something. That was the old maid's impression at least, and gradually she harbored a sort of tenderness mingled with dread for Blanchonnet.

The day after the baroness died, Félicie arrived around nine o'clock, as usual, and heard the news from the servants. She felt then that she had lost her only friend in the house and shed tears of pity over her own misfortune; after which, she asked for a few details and revelled in the ample narrative furnished alternately or in chorus by the manservant, housemaid, and cook. Her curiosity aroused, she went off to see Madame and, trying to look even smaller than Heaven had made her, humbly begged to be allowed to kneel for a moment in the death chamber. This favor was granted without even so much as a glance at her; however, Madame added between two yawns (for she had slept very little): "And please remove that ridiculous Blanchonnet while you're there, Félicie. Monsieur le curé almost upset it on the bed. It's indecent. From now on, you and the dummy can work on the third floor, in Monsieur Jean's former room."

You and the dummy was said with a knowing smile which Félicie did not see, as she never looked Madame in the face, but the strange expression echoed through her. So much so that when she opened the door of the room where the dead woman lay, she already felt quite moved. The plum-colored velvet curtains were drawn. The only light in the room was a four-branched candlestick standing by the great black mahogany bed. A heavy smell of medicines blended with the scent of a large white bouquet on the paunchy chest of drawers where the baroness used to have her keepsakes. Papers had been burnt in the hearth, small china objects swept to one side to make room for yellow glass bottles, and the violet chintz armchair had been wheeled into a corner. This disorder seemed dreadful to the dressmaker, who dared not turn her eyes toward the dead woman's face. However, she noticed with a beating heart short hands bound together by a mother-of-pearl rosary and reposing over the bulky, rounded stomach. Her knees gave suddenly and she buried a little pointed nose in the blue eider-down quilt, murmuring reproachfully: "Oh, Madame la Baronne! Oh, Madame la Baronne!"

She really tried to pray, but the words rushed to her lips in such confusion that she did not know what she was saying. She blew her nose very softly, as though she were in church, crossed herself, sighed several times, and felt for her pince-nez that hung by a chain, for after all, as she was there, she might as well glance around her. . . . A corpse was a very strange sight and the opportunity to see one was rare. It was frightening at first, to be sure, and the dressmaker, who now bent over the bed, could not keep back an exclamation of terror. How much her old friend had changed! Could this be the kindly, garrulous woman who had joked with Félicie only two days ago? The latter felt her hands grow moist and still she could not make up her mind to leave the room. She had to fill her eyes with this sight and, in a fashion, take it away with her, in order to feast upon it later, with her friends.

A little abashed by her own impudence (for, after all, it was Madame la Baronne whom she made bold to inspect so closely), she mumbled a few confused words, as though to apologize, and rubbed her pince-nez on a corner of her black apron. It was then that she had the feeling of not being alone in the room. A little shiver of fear ran down her spine and everything grew dim. For someone stood a little behind Félicie and to her right.

For a moment or two, the dressmaker thought that she would faint, for she did not dare turn her head and what she saw from the tail of her shortsighted eye seemed appalling; then she suddenly remembered Blanchonnet. With a little cry of relief and irritation, she crossed the distance that separated her from the dummy and slapped its ostentatious black bosom. Her gesture of bravado was accompanied by a timid laugh which she immediately checked. Her knees still shook a little and she was obliged to lean against a wardrobe to recover some strength.

When her beating heart grew calmer, she decided to leave the room and take Blanchonnet with her. Throwing the door wide open so both of them could pass, she grappled with the dummy, tilted it forward, and, just as it was about to topple over her, grasped it by the middle. Then she dragged it from the room, breathless and full of resentment against that confounded wretch of a Blanchonnet that had turned so heavy, indeed as heavy as a corpse.

On the threshold, she passed a nun who had come to pray by the deceased baroness, whose piety had been the edification of many. Félicie apologized in a weary, broken voice. She did not quite know what she apologized for, but she apologized, nevertheless. Ever since childhood, she had apologized to one and all: the consciousness of being so small, the constant dread of being at fault, were at the root of this scared humility. And so, catching the nun's astonished eye, she drew in her gray head, bowed her shoulders, and looked guilty, as though she had stolen the dummy from the dead woman's room. She even tried to conceal a little of Blanchonnet by bending over it and murmured several times: "It was Madame who told me to . . ." But the nun had already closed the door.

Félicie thought that she would never succeed in lifting a great hostile dummy that seemed to wish to crush her. Yet she managed to do so and carried it to the staircase. The steps were wide and shallow, fortunately, but all the dressmaker's efforts could not prevent the big wooden stand from catching the banisters with diabolical malice. She almost slipped several times, for she walked up backwards and her legs gave way from weariness. Every minute or so, she sat down, resting her head against the wall, her short little arms clasping the dummy tight, and then, with furious energy, she resumed her struggle with Blanchonnet, stood it up as best she could, hoisting it from step to step. It was so large that it almost concealed her: all that could be seen over the dummy's shoulder was a mop of tousled gray hair and Félicie's anguished eyes, then hands that held the glossy black waist in a convulsive grip, and lastly, stumbling feet in black boots that seemed to tread a dance.

The journey was not accomplished silently, in spite of the dressmaker's efforts, for she moaned each time that Blanchonnet hit the banisters—which it seemed to do sheerly to annoy her. To the old maid's great terror, a door finally opened and someone asked what that infernal row was about, but a distant, contemptuous voice, Mme Vasseur's, broke in at that moment: "It's nothing," she said, "it's only Félicie." And the door closed a thought more gently than it had opened.

When she reached the end of her weird martyrdom, Félicie had just enough strength to push her burden into the attic, but fatigue made her so awkward and her movements so uncertain that she tipped Blanchonnet over and it fell, with a kind of calculated slowness, against a china basin and broke it in two.

The dressmaker was not even aware of the accident: a sort of dizziness made her lurch across the attic, and she had the feeling of having gone deaf and blind. Her knees gave suddenly and she found herself lying on the floor, eyes staring at a ceiling that darkened gradually as though the room were being plunged into night, and in her ears a sound that resembled the ocean's majestic roar.

Time went by, then she felt that her head was being cautiously raised. A cushion was slipped under her neck. Drops of cold water tickled her brow and temples next. She sneezed and sat up.

It took her almost a minute to realize that she had fainted and, through a mist that grew lighter and lighter, to recognize the symmetrical features bending over her. Two dark eyes gazed attentively into hers and made her squint; she tried to turn her head away, but a soft, delicately scented hand prevented her and gently pressed her cheek. Then Félicie breathed deeply once or twice and whispered:

"Madame Pauque!"

"You must keep quiet," said the latter. "I'll be back in a moment."

Once alone, the dressmaker noticed that a large travelling rug had been wrapped around her legs, a black woollen shawl over her breast and shoulders. Also, the dummy had been picked up and stood by the window. It was easy for Félicie to recognize Mme Pauque's thoughtfulness in these little attentions, for the lady was always on the lookout for some good deed to perform, some scratch to bandage, some misfortune to pity. Yet, how badly they spoke of her in the kitchen, that merciless tribunal that never absolves a reputation! Herbert, the English manservant, expressed his relentless dislike for the poor woman in terms of icy frenzy: he would have hanged her, he said, with the greatest pleasure. Neither Berthe nor Ernestine dared to voice such a horrible wish, but to "settle Madame's sister's hash" had become a sort of ideal for all three of them.

Personally, the dressmaker could not quite make out how she felt about Mme Pauque. She was afraid of her, of course, but then she was afraid of everyone in the house. At times, however, when Mme Pauque was with her, talking in that quiet voice of hers, she not only felt reassured, but almost pleased. Unfortunately, this good impression did not linger in Félicie's mind and no sooner had Mme Pauque turned her back than the dressmaker was once more filled with insuperable doubts. This vexed her, it was as though she played Mme Pauque false, and Mme Pauque had always treated her kindly, yet the fact was there and could not be reasoned. All things considered, she would have liked it better if Mme Pauque had not called on her so often and, above all, not walked in at the very moment when the dressmaker happened to be thinking about her. And still, how pleasantly she talked to Félicie. . . . You would have supposed, from her engaging conversation, that she had set her heart on winning the dressmaker's affection. She seemed constantly to forget that she was Madame's sister, never scolding, never demanding anything. It could scarcely be her fault if she was always in the way at the wrong moment, if she seemed to be keeping an eye on everyone. You turned round, and there she was. She smiled, she had not seen a thing, and she went her way, but curious remarks escaped her at times, remarks that you could not quite succeed in forgetting.

These thoughts kept the old maid busy during Mme Pauque's absence, and she felt guilty when she saw the latter return to the attic with a glass of cordial in her hand, then kneel and raise her—raise her, Félicie, a dressmaker employed by the Vasseurs—to make her swallow a delicious liquid that smelt of orange and burnt sugar.

"Do you feel better, my poor Félicie?"

How lovely she looked as she said this! Her white forehead framed in black hair that shone like ink, her deep still eyes, every bit of her long face was radiant. The flesh fell in beneath the cheekbones and tiny wrinkles had begun their patient work around eyelids dark with sleeplessness; in the same way, the taciturn, secretive mouth was lightly tinged with mauve, as though a chill already crept up from heart to lips. In spite of the first unkind effects of age and bad health, the woman who bent over Félicie still kept her youthful features, a slim neck and supple figure, and there was something lively and unforeseen in her every movement. No one ever heard her come or go and she seemed always wrapped in silence, for people spoke very little in her presence. Dressed very carefully and with a certain curious elegance, she had a fondness for dark, glossy materials, black laces, and long, thin chains which she was apt to finger. More often than not, her hands, neck, and ears were decked with amethysts, and the faint scent of lilac that floated around her completed her voice and expression, like so much sweetness added to sweetness.

The last drop of cordial swallowed, Félicie wanted to lie down again, for she already experienced great and general well-being and the warmth that spread through her whole body made her feel like laughing and taking her ease, yes indeed, and even stretching, but Mme Pauque motioned her to get up.

"You feel perfectly well, don't you, Félicie?"

"Oh yes, Madame, perfectly well."

"In that case . . ." Mme Pauque picked up the pale blue cushion and stroked it lightly, "I shall put this under Mamma's head," she said after a pause.

Félicie heard these simple words, spoken in a calm, natural tone, without quite understanding them, but later, when she thought them over, they filled her with anxiety. Why? She could not have said why. It was just a vague impression, but a lasting one. It seemed to Félicie that she had been associated with the dead woman and, in the dressmaker's eyes, the harmless blue cushion became the instrument of some magical process.

Months went by and the old baroness faded from everyone's memory. It was discovered that she had really left this world many years before her death, for we all die when our youth leaves us and what survives is merely a wretched body that assumes our voice, our glance, our movements. At all events, that was the opinion of M. Jean, who was interested in literature, but Félicie did not enter into such niceties. To her mind, the baroness had died when her asthmatic breath no longer heaved her stomach and flabby bosom, but dead she was and would never be seen again.

That might be. All alone in her attic, where the silence was at times so deep the rustle of a silk filled Félicie's heart with alarm, she turned such memories over in her mind and asked herself questions. Do the dead return to haunt us, yes or no? When she was alive, Madame la Baronne claimed that they did. Félicie only hoped that she would not return in person to furnish her with extra information!

One night, Félicie dreamt that Blanchonnet appeared to her. This was not the first time that the dummy had disturbed the poor woman's sleep, but it usually just crossed the room, skimming over the floor. It did not speak. How could Blanchonnet have opened its lips? That night, however, it had suddenly grown a head and a couple of arms: the head and arms of Madame la Baronne, in fact.

Nothing could be weirder than her moonlike face fitted on to the dummy's elegant bust, and, to be truthful, the old lady's head seemed to suffer from vertigo, for she closed her eyes and frowned. Her fat hands came out of wide lace sleeves that looked like chicken wings, and from time to time, her fingers moved restlessly as though to catch hold of something. The dressmaker soon realized that the apparition was coming toward her, swaying from right to left, and, with each of Blanchonnet's movements, the baroness' cheeks quivered and the old lady cried: "Oh!" At a very short distance from the bed, the dummy stopped, its mouth opened, and Félicie drew the sheet over her head. In spite of this, she heard someone call her by name, but softly, as the baroness used to call her. She then uncovered half of one eye and looked at her mistress.

"My pale blue cushion," said the baroness.

Félicie's teeth chattered in reply.

"I want that cushion," said the baroness in a sharper tone.

There was a pause, then the pale blue cushion appeared suddenly in the baroness' hands. The old lady smiled.

"I'm taking it with me," she said, "but I'll lend it to you now and then, if you like. Let's be going. Oh!"

And Blanchonnet took her off, swaying from side to side.

Next day, Félicie had some difficulty in settling down to her work. Blanchonnet was just as alarming, whether it stood behind or in front of her. It seemed better to keep an eye on it. She placed it at her right because it stood in her light, on her left, but in both cases, the dummy inconvenienced her. She finally turned her back on Blanchonnet.

She would have felt easier if the street had not been so quiet, if a ragman had gone by, if a dog had given tongue, and if the sky had not turned the ugly gray that meant rain. Although it was nearly noon, the attic was dark and the dressmaker bent so low over her work that her nose all but touched the puce silk petticoat she had been given to mend, Madame's petticoat. This rich woman's garment aroused her jealousy and anger, but she really had no motive for working herself into a state over Madame. Reasons of prudence and self-interest alone prevented her from tearing the petticoat to pieces, with wide, sweeping gestures. She was afraid.

When she sewed, she usually hummed a sentimental

ditty in which yearning brought spurning and heart somehow rhymed with never part. Or she talked to herself, complained to Blanchonnet that life was no joke, nor was it an easy matter, but that morning, she kept an angry silence. In a moment, when she had put the last stitch to the petticoat, she would have to get up and try it on the dummy to make sure that the mend was concealed in the pleats of this disdainful garment. She intended to knock that fool of a Blanchonnet about because he had played a prank on her the night before, and she stitched faster and faster, as though she were fighting for time.

She was too much absorbed to hear the door open and started on seeing Mme Pauque.

"Nervous as ever," said the latter with a pleasant smile. "What would you do if someone really unexpected came in? For instance . . ." She sat down and clasped long hands sparkling with rings. ". . . the devil, for instance!" she said softly.

Félicie shrank back and began to laugh, merely from politeness, for she did not care for her visitor's jokes. A few seconds went by during which both women indulged in a fit of spurious gaiety, then Mme Pauque added:

"Make yourself easy on that score, my dear Félicie. It would show great ignorance to credit the devil with an ugly appearance. He does his best to please us and nothing in the world could induce him to cause us the least alarm. So he only shows himself to us under pleasant aspects, sometimes, alas, under attractive ones. . . . But we're jesting over serious matters, Félicie. I came to tell you about one of my niece's ideas."

Fingering her chain, she explained to the dressmaker that Ulrique wanted to give a party in honor of her cousin, little Hedwige. It was thought, at first, that a reception would be sufficient, but one of Ulrique's whims had reduced this reasonable plan to nothing. She wanted music, a band. She wanted a ball and it had to be a fancy-dress ball. The cost of this caprice had been pointed out to her vainly; her husband had been particularly vehement in his protestations, but it was a waste of time and trouble to argue with her, for by opposing her fancies, whatever had been so far undecided or cloudy became firmly established in her mind. She did not lose her temper, but listened to the harshest criticism with crushing politeness, and her only expression was one of icy stubbornness. In Ulrique, the only sign of anger was unusual composure. She never articulated more clearly, nor weighed her words more carefully, than in moments where other people lost their self-control. It seemed as though fury made her lucid and, in a sense, exalted her.

In her conversation with Félicie, Mme Pauque did not even allude to the almost daily scenes caused by Ulrique's plan. As she was naturally untalkative, and much opposed to confidences, when these confidences were not addressed to equals, she limited her explanations to a few sentences pronounced in the pleasant well-modulated voice that made every word music.

"Have you understood me, Félicie? Don't be frightened by this little extra work. We will pay you double for the time you spend on the costumes. How is your rheumatism?"

The dressmaker satisfied her visitor's curiosity on this point and even prepared thoughtlessly to give a few details concerning the different aspects of her health, for she was passionately interested in her little body's ailments, when Mme Pauque suddenly remembered that someone was waiting for her on the first floor.

Once she was alone, Félicie steadied the pince-nez on her nose and grew quite pink as she thought of what she might have told Mme Pauque if the latter had not staved off such indiscretions. She turned to Blanchonnet and, forgetting the grudges she bore this worthy, murmured: "Blanchonnet, what a good thing it is that you were there to prevent Félicie from talking nonsense. You're sharper than she is, you never open your lips."

She stopped suddenly and said in a louder voice: "Whatever are you saying, you old lunatic? There you go, talking to yourself again!"

She turned her back testily on the dummy and took up her work again.

Chapter 2

The house took up a long area between the street and an old-fashioned garden enclosed by extensive latticework. Above the front door was a partly obliterated coat of arms where a curly head, a crescent of the moon, and, in one corner, something that resembled a bird could still be distinguished, but most people made no attempt to decipher this haughty riddle; enough for them to know that these were armorial bearings, and, in some unaccountable manner, the fact gave them a better opinion of themselves, and such was the virtue of the escutcheon that certain inhabitants of the old house felt themselves a trifle superior to the rest of the world. "It seems to me," one of these persons remarked occasionally, "that the bearings in our coat of arms crumble away a little more, month by month, and soon nothing will be seen of it." "Never mind," lazy Ulrique would reply, "it's one of the best known in this part of the world, and its meaning will always be clear enough."

This remark, made very languidly, betrayed a somewhat justified pride, for the said escutcheon went back four centuries and what harm was there in speaking of "our coat of arms" when the magnificent ornament that beautified the façade had been bought, along with the dark, tumble-down dwelling? As a matter of fact, the Vasseurs found it difficult to get used to their house and it still awed them, after ten years of occupancy: the vaultings were too lofty, the staircase too majestic, and the drawing rooms too vast. It seemed impossible to warm up the walls, or to put new life into what wished to die in a house where even the great windows seemed contemptuous. Sofas threw themselves back and opened their arms before the fireplaces; brigades of chairs assembled in corners; round tables blocked openings, but all in vain: one element remained to frustrate the decorators' every wile: sheer emptiness.

Bernard Vasseur was unaware of this. He was a good, simple man who wanted everything to be for the best, but who realized dimly that he made himself ridiculous at least three times a day. For this reason, he kept silent before strangers and merely smiled when Ulrique's friends spoke to him. He was a little over fifty when, in the presence of a notary, he signed a deed against which both his heart and reason protested, and sighed as he murmured: "Now I'm a man of property. . . ." "For life," added his wife, taking a handkerchief from her handbag as though to conceal a smile of joy. He began to age from that day. He stooped under an invisible burden, and his daughter made no bones about telling him that he was as round-shouldered as the telamones of their monumental mantelpiece, at the other end of their drawing room. "But that's where my comparison stops," she said with a mocking smile, "for in other respects, you aren't in the least alike!" "Ulrique," said Mme Vasseur calmly. "Come now, she's right," he answered, drawing himself up slightly. "I've never been good-looking. I've inherited my father's good health, but my father wasn't handsome. A man doesn't need to be handsome." "Oh, Papa!" protested Ulrique. None the less, he shook his head and walked to a badly lit corner of the huge room where his daughter concealed his tobacco jar, of which she was ashamed, and his newspaper, which she thought vulgar, "a paper for concierges." And there, in an armchair turned to the wall, he built himself a kind of shelter against his enemy the house, which he called the historical monument when he wanted to annoy his wife and daughter. He lit a meerschaum pipe on which, to Ulrique's and Mme Vasseur's great embarrassment, a naked woman stuck out her stomach, then he opened his newspaper, held it at arm's length, and a few minutes after, the paper wall collapsed suddenly and a smoking pipe dropped gently on the fine flowered carpet.

This accident always drew the same shriek of anguish from Mme Vasseur, who flew to rescue her precious Aubusson and pick up the pipe with a disgusted expression. Her pitiless eye watched her dozing husband's exhausted face as she wondered what madness could have possessed her to bestow herself on that little man, and there her memory tricked her, for she had not bestowed but sold herself to him, before witnesses, and for a very large sum. True enough, sleep did not improve M. Vasseur's appearance. A bald forehead, thin cheeks seamed by age, and a skin flecked with brown spots made him look as though he had been exposed for a very long time to bad weather—that was Ulrique's opinion, at least—and his mouth fell open slightly when he began to snore. Then, it seemed as though he felt his wife's gaze weighing on him: for he moved his head, and raised his eyebrows with a pained expression that might perhaps have softened a heart less full of resentment, but Emma held too many things against him to be touched by her husband's wrinkles and fatigue.

"My goodness," she said, joining her daughter, who

had not budged. "I've made you run an awful risk, child. Think, you might have looked like him!"

"Make yourself easy, Mamma," said Ulrique one day, puffing at her cigarette. "It's quite clear that you concentrated all your thoughts on Georges Attachère, at the right moment."

"How dare you say such things to your mother?" asked Mme Vasseur feebly.

"You should have married Georges Attachère," said Ulrique relentlessly, as she wrapped herself in a cloud of smoke.

"Maybe you're right," replied Mme Vasseur with a sigh, "but my hand was forced."

This conversation continued for some time before a big log fire which grew so hot that the two women gradually moved to a more temperate part of the room. Mme Vasseur sat on a sofa and her daughter on the arm of this enormous piece of furniture while the subject of Emma's marriage with M. Vasseur was once more perseveringly discussed. Mme Vasseur came off badly when she attempted to justify herself to Ulrique because she was afraid of her. She dreaded the disdainful air with which her daughter sometimes eyed her, particularly at moments when Georges Attachère's name cropped up. The poor woman thought that Ulrique would never forgive her for having resisted that paragon of masculine beauty.

"He wasn't as good-looking as that," she wailed. "You don't see him as he really was."

"What are you talking about? And what about all those photographs? Don't you suppose I'm a good judge?"

"I don't care to know about that," she whispered, with a guilty look.

With a few variations, this scene took place several times a month, for it seemed as though Ulrique was determined to make her mother pay for a mistake which she considered a serious one. She hounded Mme Vasseur with questions as soon as they were alone. In a studiously modulated voice, she tried remarks on her victim, as an executioner might have prodded at raw flesh with his knife.

She was a tall, slender woman, straight as an arrow, cool and sparing of gestures. Wide, unblinking green eyes with black lashes lent her face a weird, almost animal charm that forcibly arrested attention. Her hair, like a flood of ink, played in motionless ripples around a stubborn little brow. She unconcernedly showed her beautiful white arms and shoulders and often looked down at her hands or breast with an absent, vain expression, gazing with a pout of boredom at a camellia-soft skin. How is it she's so beautiful? wondered Mme Vasseur. Neither my mother nor I ever had such a bust, such wrists and ankles. Her nose reminds me of mine, only finer, and her mouth is like mine too, but better drawn. Her cheeks haven't the rather stupid roundness mine had, when I was her age. She is perfect. Her face has nothing to fear from the wrong light that tries to find some blemish to underline, a wrinkle to predict. You'd think that both light and shadow are infatuated with her. I'll tell her so. No, I won't, she'd be even more unkind to me.

Mme Vasseur's features still retained some traces of beauty, but they only lingered to stress the melancholy ravages of time. Her white face suffered from the sort of petrification that nature undertakes at the first signs of age and completes on our deathbed. As vitality ebbs in eyes and lips, the expression hardens and the flesh seems to grow stiff and solid, as it might under an icy blast. Mme Vasseur was fully aware of this banal disaster and patched herself up as best she could, in her daughter's interest, for there was a difference of thirty-two years between them.

"You should have had me when you were twenty," said Ulrique.

"But just think, you would be twelve years older now."

It's unfair, thought Ulrique. I'll be an old lady's daughter when I'm thirty. And she added aloud: "I won't have you wear that powder, Mamma. It's not even fit for a mason to use for mixing mortar."

It was not in Mme Vasseur's nature to resist such a peremptory order: she threw away the obnoxious powder and bought another kind. She obeyed her daughter without the least humiliation; quite to the contrary, she felt a peculiar satisfaction in arousing her tyrant's whims, even though she consequently ill-treated her husband or little Hedwige; she also kept her hand in by bullying the unfortunate Félicie with the ferocity inherent to rather cowardly natures. Some days, she was all violence. Fifty-five years on earth had not quenched her youthful propensity for evil which assumed every aspect of anger, from perfidious irony to words that rushed to her lips, words actuated by rage, and, to some extent, inspired ones. In such moments of frenzy, she knew only too well that she rose again in Ulrique's estimation. Kindness in any shape aroused Ulrique's suspicions, just as she thought every form of gentleness to be the unfailing sign of a vulgar heart. "It's our Italian blood," Mme Vasseur would explain, as she grew calmer. True enough, on her mother's side she had a

Neapolitan ancestor whose profession remained an unfathomable mystery. Nevertheless, Mme Vasseur had a dual nature, and in her heart of hearts languished a kindly mother of a family who would have liked to grow old peacefully with her knitting and a pot of herb tea, but this abortive character made way for a tigress who was not always quite sure when and what she would roar. Be it as it may, the drawing room never rang with shriller screams, never were so many doors banged in the house as the evening when Ulrique decided that a ball must be given in little Hedwige's honor. At the first signs of the coming storm, M. Vasseur took shelter in his bed, as a tired old dog runs to his kennel. "Why squabble," he murmured, slipping between his sheets, "when I'll be the one to pay for everything, when all is said and done? Have I refused to? Have they even asked me about it?"

Such simplicity of mind would have made Mme Vasseur smile, had she heard her husband's words. True, money counted very little for her: she took her daughter's side, as a matter of course, and the point was to humiliate Raoul before Ulrique, because she resented the fact that her son-in-law came of a better family than she did, and she suspected him of making fun of "old Ma Vasseur" with his friends. He had never called her by any such name, yet she thought she could read the term on the young man's lips, so much she dreaded that he judged her to be common. He puts me in the same boat with my husband, she thought sorrowfully. She was certainly better born than Vasseur, but grew confused over her great-grandfathers, whereas Raoul, without laying claim to a title, could mention among his ancestors a member of Parliament, who had flourished under the French Regency, or a magistrate that King Louis the Eighteenth had honored by the gift of a snuff-box. Both the member of Parliament and the magistrate prevented Mme Vasseur from sleeping peacefully. She guessed the moment when her son-in-law would mention these persons' names and vainly searched her brain for an answer. She could talk about her Italian blood, of course, but that was not sufficient: she preferred to insult Raoul.

Ulrique never intervened between her mother and husband when wordy battles brought them to grips. She merely said in a sentence or two what she had decided to do and lit a cigarette with the coolness of a keeper who has just thrown a hunk of meat into a bear pit. What happened next did not interest her; in such moments, she immersed herself once more in a sort of inner dream where no one had ever followed her and, with a faraway look, watched the pair of them grow redder and redder and more and more ridiculous.

The evening when the topic of the ball was fought out, Ulrique took herself to a corner of the drawing room and played patience on a console while her mother waved her short arms and Raoul described a wide circle around her, as though he intended to devour her, finally. In three minutes, thought Ulrique, Raoul is going to stamp and Mamma to shriek like a concierge. These previsions came true. Raoul showed so little self-control that he stamped five or six times, and Mme Vasseur, in the accents her daughter had foretold, declared that she had never been treated so disrespectfully as that evening, and that no one was going to stamp in her presence.

"Why not?" asked Raoul, with another stamp.

Well fed, long in the body and short-legged, he tried,

by means of a small red toothbrush mustache, to give a martial air to a round face suffused with blood made too rich by excellent meals. He usually dressed in black with a high stiff collar that made him look ceremonious and, in a way, completed his personality. One of his familiar gestures was to run his fingers over the top of his head, as though to make sure that his last remaining locks of yellow hair were still there.

Had he been alone with his wife, he would never have stormed and gestured absurdly, but Mme Vasseur tried his patience to breaking point and it relieved him a little to treat her in a high and mighty manner. It was a slight revenge for Ulrique's contempt and her silences: he dared not say a word to his wife.

"Raoul!" cried Mme Vasseur. "If I were a man, you wouldn't dare behave like this in my presence. Don't touch me!" she added, for he threw his arms up and she pretended to be afraid he would strike her.

Leaving her armchair with surprising agility and picking up at one swoop her bag, fan, and book of devotions, she strode through the drawing room so rapidly that the ends of her scarf flew.

"Anyway," she said, as she left the room, "you've lost, and the ball will come off. I'll tell my husband about it tonight."

She stared at the door for a second and grasped the knob with a shaking hand. Ulrique stopped her ears. There was a brief silence immediately followed by a crash like an explosion, and the drops on the chandelier shook like leaves in the breeze as they tinkled against each other.

"No one can shut a door like your mother," said Raoul in an expressionless voice.

This remark aroused no comment. He picked up a

small tortoise-shell box that lay within his reach and seemed about to grind it under his heel, then, changing his mind, he put it down gently on a round table.

"Good night," he murmured and went out, closing the door behind him as one shuts a sickroom door.

A Renaissance ball, thought Ulrique. Gaston and Marcel will be in white, with black slashed sleeves. René in blue and red.

Chapter 3

JEAN WAS NEVER to be met except in the winding staircase that led to his room, or sometimes in the library, but never in the drawing room or in any of the rooms where Ulrique could be found. For this proud, sensitive man watched over his privacy, as a dragon guards a treasure. In order to avoid his cousin, he took his meals in distant restaurants whose whereabouts he never revealed to a soul, and how he spent his time remained an enigma that everyone had given up even attempting to solve.

Hedwige was fond of him because, of all the men she knew, he was the only one who did not make love to her. And so she imagined that he had a secret passion, of which she herself was perhaps the object. More wily than Ulrique or less indifferent, she occasionally succeeded in surprising Jean as he went up to his room.

"My bear!" she cried theatrically, as she clung to his arm. "I won't let you go until you tell me what you're hiding in your pocket. What's that parcel?"

He wrenched himself free with a brusqueness that she pretended to think adorable.

"You're the most loving of men, at heart," she said.

She shook her curls and laughed a trifle too loud. One evening, as she clung gracefully to him, he shook her off so roughly that she had to cling to the banisters to keep from falling and stood in utter bewilderment while he locked the door of his room. What strength of mind he has, she thought. He's really somebody. . . .

She had lived with the Vasseurs since childhood. Everyone wheedled and spoilt her because she was an orphan. She was considered charming and her whimsicalness amused everyone to such an extent that after ten years, not one of her movements was the least bit natural. The family's unconscious tyranny obliged her to assume a constantly fantastic attitude from which she was never allowed to depart, for by general demand, she had to be all freaks and caprices, and her most commonplace remarks raised a smile.

Ulrique was the only one to look bored amidst the general good spirits produced by "little Hedwige." She attracted the orphan for this reason, as contempt exerts a mysterious influence over irresolute natures, but when she saw the overpink, overblonde Hedwige frisk toward her, wriggling with happiness like a pug dog, she turned her face to the wall or left the room. Hedwige then felt a kind of shock go through her, and suddenly was in no mood for laughter.

She was short and built a trifle too solidly to play the imp, a role that had been forced upon her, but was lively and blooming. Her complexion, a lovely, firm, healthy skin, grew shiny in moments of excitement, and this, in spite of all Mme Vasseur's care; the latter took a powder puff from her bag and, when she judged fitting, turned her niece into a clown.

"Your face is shiny!" she would cry, running up to the girl.

Hedwige would turn her fat, innocent cheeks toward her and close her eyes.

Mme Vasseur began looking for a husband for her young relative with the same zeal that she displayed in powdering her face, and with scarcely more thought. The truth was that, as she had never known how to use her eyes or reasoning powers, the first man who offered would have seemed to possess all the requisite qualities, but in spite of all, the old scatterbrain had lucid moments when she entertained doubts concerning her own judgment and then allowed herself to be guided by Ulrique. The interested party had no idea of the future that was being prepared for her, as it stood to reason that such an irresponsible person could not be consulted. "I know what will suit Hedwige," Ulrique would mutter between her teeth.

Ulrique stared at one and all with icy impudence and never came into a drawing room without bringing with her a vague but irritated feeling of embarrassment that gradually turned to hatred. She looked at men like a recruiting sergeant. Standing with her head thrown back slightly, she examined them through lashes heavy with mascara and mentally classed them in very clearly defined categories. The first, which was also the most numerous, comprised the old, the sickly, the bald, the fat, the thin, and all those that she summed up in one word as impossible. Next came a confused phalanx that included, helter-skelter, every man who was neither deformed nor too elderly. This part of humanity was the only one to which Ulrique directed her attention, for she hoped that by searching thoroughly among the "possibles" she might finally discover the ones that she wished to have at her feet. Like all those who consider themselves cynical, she was strangely gullible, endlessly pursuing the dreams of adolescence when she was almost twenty-four, living far less on earth than in faraway regions to which her troubled sensuality constantly harked back. Depressed by the ugliness of the faces around her, she took refuge in a kind of secret Olympus. Perhaps she herself knew nothing of this, or perhaps she did not wish to know it, for she hated the truth and only found peace in a private, morbid meditation. She was constantly returning mentally to the great herd of indecent bodies with which she peopled her brain, and for Ulrique, who was in love with phantasms, life was only real so far as it corresponded with a very clearly defined dream. This circumstance did not occur as often as she would have liked, and consequently she was at times tragically unbalanced, although none of this appeared on the surface, beyond a wild, disdainful melancholy.

It amused her, for a time, to look for a husband for little Hedwige. Not that she worried much over her cousin's happiness, but she regarded this kind of manhunt as her particular concern. So she cast a fine, rather shortsighted, and roving eye over drawing rooms where she considered that game was plentiful. It was easy enough to choose for someone else. And as she often said to her mother in a curious hissing accent caused by the fact that she spoke with her teeth almost clenched so that the *s* could scarcely pass her lips: "I know exactly what will suit Hedwige."

The winter went by and the plan for the Renaissance ball was dropped just when everyone had rallied to it, to the extent of discussing whether it would not be better to adopt the early part of the sixteenth century as costumes were of greater elegance then than at its close. They had even gone so far as to consult Jean, who knew all about the particulars of this period's styles, and the unfortunate dressmaker was already at work on crimson silk that blurred her eyesight, when Ulrique, finding everyone in agreement, at last decided that the whole business was really a bore and that a simple reception would do just as well. The truth was that she had dreamt about the ball for weeks, dressed and undressed too many elegant young men in their silks and velvets. Having exhausted this pleasure, nothing remained to her but a certain distaste for life and extreme contempt for what she mentally termed "the whole tribe of 'em"; for her mother pictured herself as Louise of Savoy, and Raoul, suddenly won over to the ball, aspired to nothing less than appearing as Francis the First. Then, thought Ulrique, the whole thing became impossible. No ball. Mme Vasseur cried and gave in. Raoul spoke very firmly and declared he would assert his authority but, as usual, did nothing of the sort. No ball. The crimson silk could be used to cover the drawing-room cushions.

And so, one Sunday in April, a reception was held at the Vasseurs' and the young man intended as a husband for Hedwige put in a somewhat timid appearance toward the end of the afternoon. Without being handsome, he had the robust, healthy looks of a man of the people. His light eyes glanced slyly this way and that under heavy eyebrows, and his thick lips parted at times—not to speak, for he never had anything to say—but to show his square and dazzling white teeth. Now and again, with a rather awkward gesture, he pushed back his curly hair, a tangle of ringlets over his low brow, or touched his powerful neck with a single finger as though to free himself from an unbearably stiff collar. He stood near the door and had a fair chance of not being noticed when he saw fit to leave. About forty people gossiped around him, but Ulrique spotted him as soon as he came. What a charming little workman! she thought. She swam up to him.

That he was not in his proper place and suffered in

consequence gave Ulrique visible satisfaction; nothing pleased her more than false situations. She noted that her guest not only provoked some slight astonishment, but also a vague disapproval, as though it were ill-bred to have such high coloring and such broad shoulders. The stranger felt this tacit disapprobation keenly: his whole person exuded a somewhat animal seductiveness, of which he himself was fully aware at that moment, as though it was a disgrace.

Ulrique omitted introducing him to the old ladies who drew away as they passed by them and led him to a corner of the drawing room where her cousin was complacently responding to the advances of a general in mufti. She interrupted this philandering by pinching Hedwige's arm.

"I have someone here that I want you to meet," she whispered quickly. "Take my advice: don't talk so loud. Don't show your gums when you laugh, and put a little powder on, from time to time." Aloud, she said: "Monsieur Gaston Dolange."

A few minutes later, as she was ostentatiously yawning at the other end of the room, Ulrique saw Hedwige squeezing her way through groups of people and advancing toward her with the air of someone who had been caught in a brawl.

"What's the matter?" asked Ulrique, leading her cousin to a window recess.

"That young man . . . I didn't catch his name . . . why did you introduce him to me? Who is he?"

"He's the son of a merchant at Nantes. Your nose is shiny. You're out of breath. Pull yourself together and tell me what the matter is."

"I don't want to see that young man again."

"Ah? What's he done?"

"Nothing," said Hedwige, rubbing her face with her handkerchief. "He's very dull and . . . very ugly."

The last words were said in a tearful voice, but Ulrique knew how to cut this display of feeling short.

"Your forehead has a wonderful polish," she said, lighting a cigarette. "I wouldn't shine it up further, if I were you."

The handkerchief dropped from Hedwige's hand.

"What's his name?" she asked.

He has turned her head and she is frightened, thought Ulrique. It's perfectly fantastic. Let's give the girl a name she can sigh out, in private.

"Gaston," she replied, after a short pause. "Gaston Dolange."

Hedwige looked intensely grateful.

"So you think he's very ugly?" asked Ulrique.

Hedwige quivered, as though she had been roused from a dream.

"Yes," she said. "He looks like a young ogre. I don't want to see him again."

Ulrique looked at her for almost a minute, in silence, with the impassive expression that made her seem so lovely and so hateful too, then, suddenly throwing away her cigarette, she caught Hedwige by the wrist.

"You little fool," she whispered in her ear. "What do good looks signify? Young Dolange has far more than that!"

Things followed their natural course, which means that M. Dolange, thinking perhaps that he had not found favor, was seen no more and that Hedwige began to experience all the languishments of love as described in the ditties hummed by Félicie. This promises to become extremely dull, thought Ulrique. I'll have to fish up that burly young man again.

She felt rather proud of her success, and only half bored as she listened to the confidences her cousin treated her to, but found it difficult to explain M. Dolange's bashfulness. That Hedwige had not succeeded in fascinating him, what more natural? But what about herself? She did not want him, but yet expected the compliment of an ineffectual attempt, a petition, spoken or unspoken, a glance, something, a letter, yes, a letter; why didn't he write? The most timid men ventured to make her a declaration. He had not. Strange. "It bothers me a little on Hedwige's account," she said to herself, secretly vexed. And she added: "He must be hairy as a bear."

"Oh, how you get on my nerves!" she cried one day, as Hedwige melted into tears before her. "Is it my fault if you didn't know how to talk to young Dolange?"

"But I didn't know I was in love with him," replied Hedwige, hiding her face in some silky material that trailed over a chair.

"What! You're wiping your eyes and nose on my scarf!"

"I'm unhappy," wailed Hedwige's muffled voice.

"You're more ridiculous than anything else," said Ulrique as she snatched away her scarf.

She watched her cousin with an air of contempt and was on the verge of carelessly making the kind of remark that caused her dearest friends to dread her. You're the kind that cries, she thought; you'll never get anything. She looked at Hedwige's back that bent under a load of sorrow. Victims never get anything. However, she remained silent and, with a kind of sudden inspiration, went to the grand piano that took up a corner of the room. She threw herself, rather than sat down, on the stool and immediately began to play. A few muffled notes rose through the silence, followed by a great, mysterious chord that seemed to reach them from the heart of the earth, and very soon Ulrique's voice mingled with the instrument's deep vibrations. A weird chant arose, both gentle and solemn, tearless, quiet but calm and scornfully despairing. All the tedium of life crept into this melodious soliloquy, the long lament of a soul that only longed for death and moaned in its bodily prison as though it had been walled up there.

Ulrique stopped suddenly. She did not know why she had sung this piece, nor did she know why she ceased, but turned to Hedwige who was listening attentively and smiling.

"Go to bed, my little Hedwige," she said. "You'll meet your Dolange again this week. I'll see to it myself."

Chapter 4

"Children," announced Mme Vasseur with her unerring instinct for having a good idea at the wrong moment, "Hedwige is going to act the sad letter and the gay letter for us. Or is it the gay letter and the sad letter? Ah! I can't remember. . . . Has anyone seen my keys? No, here they are. Now, Hedwige, we're all attention. You'll see," she said, leaning toward Mme Attachère, who was spending the evening with them, "it's really very funny. That child has a real gift. . . ."

"Your mother is a magician," Raoul addressed his wife, who turned her head away. "With one word, she takes us to the heart of the most remote province."

"Hush!" cried Mme Vasseur from the other end of the room. "Now, Hedwige!"

Hedwige left her seat most reluctantly and stood under the chandelier. Her pale gray taffeta dress bared a throat heaving with sighs and plump arms that she did not know what to do with, for it seemed to her that she suddenly owned six of them, like an Oriental divinity. Without feeling shy, Hedwige had the vague impression that she was surrounded by a certain amount of malice. She had made M. and Mme Vasseur laugh many a time by "doing" the sad or the gay letter for them. It was a sort of *number* taught her by a schoolmate from the *lycée* at Troyes and stated to be extremely funny. In her provincial ignorance, the poor girl performed it with disarming willingness as often as she was asked and secretly congratulated herself over the shouts of laughter raised by her little dumb-show act. The Vasseurs, who were scarcely less ingenuous than she, thought her brilliant. Ulrique's innate cruelty prevented her from telling Hedwige that she held herself up to ridicule, and encouraged her to make a fool of herself instead. But for the last few weeks, Hedwige had suspected something: she thought that Raoul laughed too loudly and Ulrique's icy smile perplexed her.

Her task, that evening, was to amuse the guest. Seated between M. and Mme Vasseur, as though she were at a play, the mother of handsome Georges Attachère had the face of an overbearing old buccaneer much tanned by the wind and a liver complaint. Gold rings in her ears and a silk handkerchief knotted around her skull emphasized this unintentional likeness. Her stomach bulged under a flowered dress, and she fanned herself with a sweeping, virile gesture, wielding a bouquet of ostrich feathers with great energy, jingling chain bracelets and cabochons on her wrists. She seemed determined not to share the Vasseurs' opinion of Hedwige's talents and looked straight ahead of her, oppressively hostile.

Hedwige began by the gay letter. Holding an imaginary sheet of paper in her hand, she bent her pretty head over it and laughed softly, now and then.

"What's she doing?" asked Mme Attachère in an undertone. "I don't understand," she added, with her Central European accent.

"She's pretending to have received an amusing letter and she's reading it," explained Mme Vasseur.

"If the letter is amusing, why doesn't she read it out loud?"

This question obtained no reply. Hedwige continued to guffaw, in a mournful silence, her shoulders shaking with mirth; she turned a page, remained serious for a few seconds, then suddenly went off again into fits of shrill laughter that rocked her little body; at last, toward the end of the letter she showed her gaiety by yelps of joy, but her gaiety found no echo, for the Vasseurs felt embarrassed by Mme Attachère's silent disapproval.

They don't realize it's over, thought Hedwige, throwing in a few extra peals of laughter.

"That's excellent, most amusing," said M. Vasseur, applauding. "Don't you think so, Madame?"

"I think it very curious," replied Mme Attachère in a loud, cutting voice.

"Isn't it?" murmured Mme Vasseur, faintheartedly. "It's not quite as funny as I thought, after all, but then, we also have the sad letter."

"How many letters are there, in all?" demanded the guest.

Mme Vasseur motioned vaguely, as though to apologize for her young relative who had already begun to read the sad letter. Hedwige found it easy this time to express sentiments which she did not have to feign. It was no effort for her to imagine the harsh, contemptuous note she might receive in answer to a love letter. The illusion was so powerful that Hedwige felt as though she held the note in her fingers and her hands began to shake. Wasn't silence enough for M. Dolange? Did he have to carry cruelty so far as to disclose the reasons for his aversion to her? He refused Hedwige, he thought her too stupid and too proud. She stifled a moan of distress at the idea of her own clumsiness, for he had stood by her for at least five minutes without her finding anything to say to him, without its having even occurred to her to smile, and taking advantage of a second when he had turned his head, she had run away from him. Why? She did not know why, but tears, real tears rolled down her cheeks and wet her lips; raising a handkerchief to her mouth, she began to sob.

"That's not half bad," declared Mme Attachère, throwing herself sideways in her armchair to laugh comfortably and, opening a large mouth, showed a row of strong, yellow teeth. Her noisy laughter rose in jerks from her voluminous bosom and, as though to further this process, she stamped her heel on the carpet. Mme Vasseur gave a little nervous bleat, but her husband kept silent. As for Ulrique, she had come close to Mme Attachère by slow degrees and looked at her attentively, trying to detect in the old woman's hilarious face the features of a man Mme Vasseur had nearly married.

Meanwhile, Hedwige could not stop crying and dropped into a chair, suffocating. Mme Attachère's enormous laugh filled the drawing room and rang in the girl's ears with the savage persistence of a bell. She wondered when this atrocious mirth would cease, when it would be discovered that her grief was not feigned. What she had kept in her heart for the past two days burst out suddenly, like a storm. Never had she suffered as much, never had anguish caught her by the throat as it did now, and she lost her head, she cried from despair and shame before a woman who split her sides with laughter. All of a sudden, she felt the prey of some irresistible force; she no longer acted of her own free will, an alien volition replaced hers. She screamed. The sound of her own voice astonished her. She had time enough to see Ulrique turn slowly toward her, then she screamed again and slipped from her chair to the carpet, as though she dropped to the bottom of an abyss.

When she recovered consciousness, her eyes met Mme Pauque's motionless face watching her gravely. The night light showed up her great dark eyes and made an amethyst necklace sparkle on her black satin bodice, for although she never appeared in the drawing room, this strange woman dressed every night as though she were going to a party and went to meet night decked out in her laces and jewels.

Hedwige did not realize where she was, at first. She breathed in the delicate scent of lilac that floated through the close air in her room, and this perfume laden with vague memories made her sad and happy at the same time. The peace and mystery of the duskiness reassured her; she also liked the comforting presence of a woman whom she did not recognize. She listened for a few seconds to the voice that called to her gently and took care not to answer immediately, in order to prolong a marvellous moment when she was not in pain, then the recollection of what had happened in the drawing room swept slowly over her and she began to moan, delivered up to a torture that was all too habitual.

"Try to sleep, my child," said a wheedling voice.

"Is that you, Aunt Hélène? Oh! I'm far too unhappy to sleep."

"Try to. It's always that much gained over . . ."

"Over what?"

There was a silence and a tinkling of jewelry as Mme Pauque fiddled with her necklaces.

"Over sadness, Hedwige," she said at last, "over long-drawn-out days."

"Over life itself, Aunt Hélène. When I think that I'm in for forty or fifty years of this, I feel so weary that I'd like to die right away."

"Hush, my child!" said Mme Pauque. "You mustn't say such a thing." She added with a quiet little laugh: "Someone might hear you."

Hedwige did not reply. There was always a dark implication in Mme Pauque's jests that it was better to leave unexplained, but Hedwige thought over the sentence she had just heard for a few minutes. She started as she felt someone press her hand and then saw her aunt leave her bedside and wander noiselessly around the room. Now Mme Pauque made sure that the curtains were closely drawn or that the logs were not burning too fast in the hearth; or else she moved the bottles on the muslin-draped dressing table, and her tall, black silhouette went from one corner of the room to the other, like a shadow. Soon, she returned to the bed and laid a handkerchief soaked in cologne on Hedwige's forehead.

"Aunt Hélène," asked Hedwige suddenly, "who could hear us?"

"How should I know?" whispered Mme Pauque, her long, cold hands furtively stroking Hedwige's cheeks. "You're too curious, my child. You must go to sleep."

Hedwige could not sleep. Too many regrets harassed her, too many thoughts to which she continually returned, urged by a curious need to suffer, to make her pain sharper. The humiliation of having cried before a stranger tortured her for some time, and to have fainted in Ulrique's presence seemed almost more serious to her.

She felt herself blush, but this disgraceful scene soon faded away, as though to make room for mental images that were richer in sadness, for she was deeply fascinated by her own sorrow. She knew none of the stratagems which a more experienced woman would have used to ward off the enemy, she surrendered without a struggle and gave herself up wholeheartedly to the cruel delights of reminiscence. Hundreds of times, over and over again in the darkness of her room, she felt compelled to summon up a young man who had nothing to say to her. There he stood before her, and she almost stretched out her hand to touch him. Sometimes, when she was tired, he vanished into a sort of fog. She would call him back then, with a great silent call of the heart; the dead hear this cry, but it was a living man whom she tried to bring back, or at least his double, that deaf and shadowy being who wanders vacantly through the dreams of unrequited love.

She remained motionless, for a long time, her hands folded over her breast, absorbed in the contemplation of this imperious apparition. "Listen," she murmured, "I want to tell you . . ." But she did not know what she wanted to tell him; she lay shivering in bed and thought that she saw a brown face with moist lips come close to her. It even seemed as though a warm breath softly touched her cheek and that someone called her insistently, in a whisper. The delusion was so strong that she grew frightened and suddenly left her bed.

"What's the matter with me?" she asked aloud. "Am I going to be ill?"

She gazed at herself in the mirror on the dressing table and thought that she looked ugly; as usual, her nose and forehead were shiny. From sheer sadness, she sank into a chair and leaned her head on the little table, among the brushes and silver-topped boxes. Something shattered within her and, for the first time in her life, she thought of the future with a kind of horror. "How do other people behave when they're in pain?" she asked herself. "Where do they find the strength to get from one hour to the other, until life is over?"

The door opened at that moment and Mme Vasseur entered with her great bustling stride, then stopped short in the middle of the room.

"Where are you?" she asked. "Why this dismal light? Hedwige! Ah! you're there. Well, how are you?"

"I'm very well," whispered Hedwige as she rose.

"I was certain of it. Hélène brought in that night light, didn't she? That's where I recognize her desire to dramatize the most commonplace situations. Now, *I* just turn on the light," she added, switching it on.

A hard, white light flashed from the ceiling and spread through the whole room. Hedwige closed her eyes.

"There," said Mme Vasseur, "and I can see, by the same token, that your face is terribly shiny, my poor little dear." And, using one of Ulrique's favorite expressions, she added: "A mason wouldn't have the kind of powder you wear to mix his wet mortar."

She fingered her bare arms inside big yellow lace sleeves and cried suddenly: "I've lost my bag!"

Her gray head tossed on a scrawny neck, a black eye stared like a panic-stricken old horse as she turned her profile right and left. In a great swishing of taffeta, she went from the room without another word, leaving the door open.

I'll go to see Ulrique, thought Hedwige. She'll tell me what to do.

This decision put fresh heart in her. She brushed her

hair, powdered her face carefully, as she knew that a close inspection awaited her, then, forcing herself to smile in the looking glass, she left the room with that expression on her face.

"Here I am," she announced, walking into Ulrique's room, "and, as you see, I feel very well."

A deep silence greeted this good piece of news. Ulrique attentively studied the cards she had laid out on the table, and for a short time did not answer her visitor.

"Sit down," she said at last, with a sigh.

The small lamp standing on the table merely showed up Ulrique's hands and the lower part of her face, for a thick shade confined the light and directed it on the ceiling, leaving the walls of the room in the dark. Outlines of furniture that gleamed like metal could be vaguely guessed at in the dimness, the plaster cast of a curly-haired classical head was faintly reflected in a black mirror.

Hedwige sat by the hearth, where two log ends smoldered. She could not make up her mind to open her lips. She always felt hideous when she was with her cousin and, even when silent, guilty of some major error against intelligence and good taste. So she was wondering why she had come when Ulrique's voice broke the silence.

"To avoid our having a tiresome conversation," she said, pushing the table back in order to cross her legs, "I'm going to do all the questioning and answering; for I'm sleepy," she added in a lower but intelligible tone. "First of all, do I know why I'm favored with this nocturnal visit? I certainly do. You want me to tell you when you'll see Monsieur Gaston Dolange again."

Hedwige could not keep from moving, when she heard the name.

"Have I had news of Monsieur Dolange?" continued Ulrique rapidly. "I have. So I wrote to him, or made Mama write? Not at all. Then who gave me the information? My friend Arlette. You don't know her but she's intimate with one of this gentleman's cousins."

These sentences, reeled off almost at a breath, ill concealed a certain embarrassment. Ulrique uncrossed her legs and stirred slightly in her armchair. She was loath to admit her unsuccess, but eager to see the effects of her remarks and, with a movement that escaped Hedwige's notice, picked up the lamp and stood it on the mantelpiece. Her cousin's face then became visible, eyes set and glittering, lips parted. A few seconds went by, then Ulrique lit a cigarette and said deliberately:

"Monsieur Dolange has gone to La Rochelle. He intends to live there."

"Ah!" said Hedwige.

She remained motionless. Her ears buzzed, drops of sweat slowly rolled down her brow. Through a sort of mist, she saw her cousin get up, tidy her hair at a mirror, sit down again, then pick up the cards and shuffle them.

"I'll let you have a little of my powder tomorrow," said Ulrique. "I don't know how you manage it, at times you look like a glass ball, the kind that can still be seen on old-fashioned lawns, and at others like a wall that has just been plastered. Here," she added, handing her the pack of cards, "shuffle them and ask whether my husband is going to die soon."

Hedwige took the cards and shuffled them with moist hands. With mechanical docility, she mentally asked the appalling question with which Ulrique pestered fate almost every day. Then she handed the cards to her cousin, who laid them out on the table. The answer was no.

"You didn't think hard enough as you asked the question," said Ulrique. "Your mind wasn't on it. Oh! you aren't going to cry, are you? I thought you showed pluck, a moment ago."

Hedwige shook her head and wiped her forehead and cheeks. She got up, seemed undecided for an instant, and then made for the door, steadying herself against the furniture.

She's overacting a bit, thought Ulrique as she shuffled the cards once more, a cigarette between her lips. It wouldn't have occurred to her, if she'd been alone, to walk like a blind woman in a melodrama. Yet, in spite of this, she must be suffering. That's odd.

When the door closed, she said aloud: "Very odd!" and sat still for a moment, staring into space, then she laid the cards on the table once more and made a gesture of impatience: the answer was still no. But Ulrique asked again and again until the cards said yes, and she went to bed, satisfied.

Hedwige's bedroom was on the floor above Ulrique's, and it sometimes happened that she was roused from sleep in the dead of night by the sound of the piano. Far from minding it, she liked to hear the muffled voice rising from below, talking to her in the dark, at times gentle and insinuating, at others passionate and aggressive. It seemed to Hedwige that the melodies continued her dreams instead of interrupting them and very soon a delightful melancholy stole over her or, according to her cousin's mood, an almost heroic enthusiasm possessed her. In the innocence of her heart, she sometimes fancied that the music was intended for her, but innate discretion prevented her ever mentioning it. The nocturnal dialogue between herself and Ulrique was Hedwige's secret. Her head still misty with dreams, she listened, entranced, to the vague, tumultuous questions tossed at her by the piano's voice and, for a few minutes, was under the illusion of having great spiritual wealth, of having been given a mysterious authority over all beings. No human words could have conveyed a clear idea of this confused but deeply rooted sensation. At such moments, Hedwige experienced the rare happiness that resembles spiritual ecstasy. Darkness aiding, she came to believe that the walls of her room vanished, that she left her body then, to fly away into night, into empty space. This peculiar happiness was not spoilt by dizziness. She went where she wished and her one desire was to flee. Her only fear was that the piano might stop before she reached the bottomless gulf of sleep where silence collapsed in a roaring of waterfalls. And if the music ended too soon, a shock went through Hedwige, as a somnambulist wakes with a sigh of terror.

That night, however, her mind was not on such things. She staggered to her bed, like a sick animal. She dreaded night, for it lasted so long, and wondered where she would find courage enough to face the day that would dawn within a few hours, then after day, another night, and an alternate succession of light and shadow that could only bring her sorrow.

At present, as she lay in bed on her stomach, face buried in the pillow and fists pressed to her temples, she tried not to think of anything, but her cousin's words swirled about in her mind: ". . . La Rochelle. He intends to live there." An hour earlier, Hedwige knew nothing about his departure and thought herself unhappy, then. Ah, she must have been mad! She should have danced with joy at the mere idea that they both of them lived in the same town, but now that they were separated by an eight-hour journey, her ordeal began in good earnest.

Turning over on her back, she whispered: "An eight-hour journey." And these words, spoken in a hesitant, broken voice, surprised her as much as if a stranger had suddenly breathed them in her ear. She lifted a hand to her shoulder to unfasten her dress and had scarcely done so when she fell asleep.

She dreamt that people hustled around her in a huge, dark, sonorous room. Indistinct words and abuse were hurled at her and she had great difficulty in forcing her way through a hostile crowd, when she suddenly found herself once more in her room and lying on her bed. I have been dreaming, she thought, lighting the little bedside lamp. She sat down to remove her shoes, for they hurt her. All of a sudden, her heart beat faster: in the window recess, half concealed by the mirror on the dressing table, someone sat on a little, low chair, and gazed at her with extraordinary attention. Hedwige remained bent double, not daring to move.

"Who are you?" she asked finally.

The reply came swiftly, without her hearing the faintest sound of words:

"Look at me."

She raised her eyes to see a shabbily dressed man smiling at her. He looked so humble that at first she took him for a beggar and wondered how he had found his way into her room, but she was not in the least afraid. On the contrary, there was something reassuring in the stranger's presence. A few minutes went by in silence, then the man pointed out a pair of nail scissors that lay on the dressing table.

"You want my nail scissors?" asked Hedwige, trying to laugh. "How funny! You can have them."

The man did not move, did not raise a finger, and the scissors disappeared. He smiled gently at her astonishment and then looked around him. His eyes fastened on a pen-and-ink drawing that hung on the wall in a gilt frame. Hedwige understood that he wanted the drawing too. I don't care for it much, she thought. He can have it, if it gives him any pleasure.

She did not have to express her consent, for the spot on the wall where the drawing had hung a second before was bare. Yet the man no longer seemed to pay Hedwige any attention and, without leaving his seat, looked from one corner of the room to another. With an almost imperceptible gesture, he finally directed her glance to a dark red velvet cape that she had laid on an armchair, and waited. She hesitated. The cape, with its ermine collar and silver clasp, had been given to her by Ulrique, who had discarded the wrap after wearing it five or six times. In Hedwige's eyes, however, nothing could be so beautiful as a cape that dressed her up with such pomp—she might have attended a coronation in it —although her native gaucherie scarcely qualified her to wear a garment of that kind. She naïvely imagined that she resembled Ulrique each time she felt the weight of the sumptuous material and the soft fur over her shoulders. So she pretended not to understand what the stranger wanted. "The cape," he said mentally to her. "No," she replied, "you're going too far." But he looked so sadly at her that she suddenly gave in. She turned her eyes away from the cape, thinking: I'll give it to him. The cape disappeared.

The man stood up presently. He was taller than Hedwige would have thought and showed a certain amount of assurance. He pointed to the things that she most cared for: the modest bits of jewelry, those of a little provincial girl who clung to her possessions, the souvenirs that she cherished as a miser cherishes his pennies. And she wrestled with the stranger, but he always won, for he had a gentle, persuasive way of asking for this and that: he wanted everything, in fact, furniture, books, love letters, and Hedwige felt as though she were losing her mind, for no sooner had these things disappeared than others immediately took their place: a painted chest of drawers that had been given her for her twelfth birthday, the bed she had slept in as a little girl, with its buttercup-yellow counterpane and muslin curtains, picture books long since destroyed or lost, the whole of a lot of charming odds and ends, that she was startled to see after so many years of oblivion. But she scarcely had time to recognize a toy, a box of paints, or some glass beads before they were taken away from her, and on each occasion she felt the same astonishment. Yet she experienced no pain; for the last few minutes, she had, on the contrary, a strange desire to give away even more, not to keep anything for herself. She felt really happy, for the first time in her life; a huge burden slipped from her shoulders and she lurched about unsteadily, like a child who has not yet learnt to stand by itself. She looked around her. The room was empty, but filled with blinding light, and then Hedwige understood that she had given away the whole of her childhood.

"There is nothing left," she said. "I am free."

The man had vanished. Yet she heard his voice say: "No."

At the same moment, Gaston stood before her. His head tilted slightly to one side, he smiled a cruel, half-serious, half-mocking smile, already certain of having triumphed. His teeth gleamed, his slanting blue eyes creased above pink cheekbones; everything in this attractively ugly face was charged with sensual happiness and a lust for love.

"Give him up and you'll be free," said the voice.

Hedwige felt a sudden violent revulsion.

"No," she said. "I can't. I want this man's love."

She had hardly said this when she found herself once more in her room, under its usual aspect, with its curtains, its furniture, its dressing table whose mirror had so often shown her the reflection of a melancholy little face. The walls seemed to close in around her, as much as to smother her. She was alone, and with a loud wail, awoke.

Could it be that she had slept only five minutes? She lit the little lamp and shook her watch, for she thought it had stopped, but the hands did not lie: it was half-past one. She tried to remember her dream and almost succeeded. She stared at the velvet cape, but the more she thought, the more everything grew confused in her mind and all that remained was an impression of extreme happiness followed by a sudden, violent blow that still pained her. Anyway, she thought, a good deal of the night has gone by.

She sat on the edge of her bed to remove her shoes and, as she stretched her hand toward her right foot, stopped, bewildered: she had already made that movement before under the same circumstances, but when? She recognized the dense silence of the little room, the light that just grazed the hem of the red cape, and in her own heart lay a feeling of despair that never left her now. There her recollections ended; something in her memory stumbled against a kind of wall; it was as though a whole side of her nature remained inaccessible to her and the fact secretly troubled her. She took off her shoes and put on slippers with the weird sensation of having broken a spell, of having gone to the right when she should have walked to the left, for now that she was up, the mystery of which she had had a glimpse faded away completely and she became what she had been: an ignorant, bewildered girl who simply wanted the happiness this world can give.

Chapter 5

THE FOLLOWING DAYS were painful for everybody. Hedwige suffered, and she suffered, it must be said, with very little self-restraint. From top to bottom of the big house, everyone knew that Hedwige was in love with a young man who, most unfortunately, would have nothing to do with her. In any case, even if she had kept her outbursts of grief for the solitude of her room, she would have been betrayed by her silence, sighs, reddened eyelids, and utter indifference to everything outside an absorbing melancholy. Meals were particularly trying. To refuse one course after the other, drink a mouthful of water with a strained expression, then stare long and desperately at the door as she nervously crumbled her bread, never to answer a question, or start when someone touched her arm: she spared her family nothing that could weary compassion, and quickly became very tiresome.

"You must try to react," murmured M. Vasseur.

React! What was the meaning of the word? There she recognized a language spoken by people who were foreign to her grief and to her love, namely, the whole world, and it gave her a slightly conceited satisfaction to feel that she was alone, absolutely alone. Sometimes, she drove back tears as they welled into her eyes, but her effort was visible and she knew it. She ostensively concealed her sorrow, so to speak.

To tell the truth, this method of making a spectacle of herself mitigated her torture, to a certain extent. The mere fact of being unhappy exalted her, in her own eyes. Until then, she had known only the petty vexations and mediocre pleasures of an unruffled existence, and now her life had suddenly changed into something truly abominable, but also passionately interesting. Fate had marked her out, she felt, and secretly pitied the serene human beings whom misfortune passed by.

These artless thoughts went to her head. She was, at last, the equal of the scornful Ulrique, whose attitude of regal displeasure she envied; meals became almost endurable as she could vie with her model in boredom. At night, however, left to herself, without an audience before whom to perform her lugubrious farce, she was once more a prey to relentless despair. In order to suffer more keenly, she often scrutinized her likeness in the mirror and asked herself endless questions concerning what M. Dolange had thought of her and what he would think of her if, through an impossible chain of circumstances, he could see her then, in the becoming light shed by the little lamp that she held up to her face, this way and that. She really looked pretty with her hair falling loose over her shoulders, and late hours had put dark rings around her eyes and made them appear bigger. Her cheeks lost their roundness and bloom. She discovered that she had an interesting face. Once, she slipped off her nightgown and gazed sadly at a youthful body that no one ever saw. What use were those lovely round arms that embraced nothing more real than the emptiness of confused and disappointing dreams, such a white, purely shaped bosom, hips where she had hoped someday to feel the soft warmth of another's hand, the weight of another's head, the freshness of another's cheek? How could it be that such a simple act was not possible? She fancied the young man at her feet, but from strange shyness, she shrank from imagining him otherwise than as she had seen him in her aunt's drawing room and, without realizing how funny it was, always addressed him as M. Dolange. For she talked to him as though he were present, she argued with this ghost, lied to him sometimes, even though she afterwards admitted it. This melancholy pastime comforted her a little, though it also frightened her. What would people think of her if they knew that she talked to herself in the silence of dawn? The idea troubled her at times and spoilt her sad pleasure, then once again the young man's face took shape as soon as she closed her eyes and she endlessly pursued this exhausting dialogue. With infinite patience, she put the same questions in a hundred different ways, laid little traps, and, according to her exacting heart, imagined M. Dolange's behavior. As time went on, she daily credited this inaccessible being with a fresh quality, and his only imperfection, to her eyes, was a childlike shyness. She was carried away by sudden impulses. She would have liked to be his mother, wife, and daughter, all in one. Her sensual desire would abruptly give way to harrowing tenderness. She would have renounced all physical pleasure, she thought, to dandle the young man like a baby, to wait on him. Then once more, she pictured his hands, his mouth, and fell back in bed, sobbing.

"How cruel you are to me!" she wailed.

She heard a knock at her door, one night, as she was writing a letter, the kind that is never sent. It's he, she thought. For a second or two, she really believed in a kind of miracle and remained silent, her eyes staring at the door, as though under the influence of some hypnotic power, but was soon undeceived by hearing Jean's voice calling her softly:

"It's I, little Hedwige. May I come in?"

She opened. He seemed to hesitate for an instant, then walked to the middle of the room and stood by the little dressing table. A worn, soiled waterproof hung to his calves and he held a shapeless, rain-sodden hat. He looked down, with a shamed expression, and bowed a great, livid brow streaked with locks of black hair.

"I saw light under your door," he said, as though to apologize. "I wanted to say good night. You don't mind my dropping in like this?"

She made a little sign as though to say no, and motioned him to a chair, but he shook his head.

"I don't want to keep you from sleeping," he said.

"Sleeping?" repeated Hedwige, as though the word had no meaning.

This time it was she who shook her head with a tragic air, but suddenly she felt embarrassed by a sharp glance from her visitor. In spite of his reserved, pleasant manners, he was not the man to be taken in and she instinctively understood that he had a contempt for the affectations with which she decked her sorrow.

A few seconds after, he sat down awkwardly on the edge of an armchair and laid his hat at his feet. His dress and something humiliated in his attitude made him look like a beggar.

"Hedwige," he said, "I wonder why I knocked at your door. It's extraordinary, isn't it? Here we are sitting together in your room and it's one o'clock in the morning."

Hedwige said nothing.

"Perhaps I have no right to come to see you at such an hour," he continued. "You probably think me disagreeable, for I've done nothing to deserve your affection, but at times my life in this house is more painful than at others: this justifies my being unsociable."

Hedwige forced a smile. She felt a little resentful that Jean should have interrupted the letter she was writing to Gaston Dolange, and also, she could not understand a word the man was saying and vaguely suspected him of leading up to a declaration of love. This sudden and sly manner of coming into her room in the middle of the night to make love to her agreed perfectly with the idea she had formed of the man she sometimes called her bear! All of a sudden, her eyes lighted on Jean's shoes: they were thickly coated with mud.

"I've been walking for hours," he said, as though in reply to the question she asked herself. "It has never stopped raining. I feel very tired and very lonely, Hedwige. That's why I wanted to see you."

"My poor bear," she murmured.

He watched her for a moment with an icy, skeptical expression which annoyed her. Never had Jean seemed more inscrutable, nor had she ever seen so much pent-up despair in a human face. Yet this despair strangely beautified him. The lamp lit up his powerful jaw and thin lips, but his dark eyes remained in the shadow, as though he looked through a mask.

"Something urged me to see you," he continued. "I feel that I must confide in someone, talk to a human being. Listen to what I'm going to tell you, but don't ask any questions."

He laid his hands on his knees and bent his head forward, then in a hurried, muffled voice he said at a breath:

"A moment ago, just five minutes from here, I was almost arrested."

Hedwige rose to her feet. "Jean!" she cried.

"Yes," he continued, "arrested in the open street, like a thief caught red-handed."

"Red-handed," she repeated.

He kept silence, watching the effects of his words on her terrified and astounded little face.

"What do you mean?" she asked finally.

"I mean that a man that I found out too late to be a police inspector followed and then accosted me, and if I had lost my nerve, I wouldn't be here, Hedwige, but at the police station. It's not a very pretty story."

"But what had you done?"

"I asked you not to question me."

"Then why are you telling me what happened to you if I'm not to understand anything about it?"

"It's precisely because you can't understand anything about it and that you'll keep it secret that I wanted to confide in you. I'm forty years old, I'm a studious man, peaceful and harmless. Yet, a short time ago, I felt that in the eyes of society, in yours too, Hedwige, I was a wicked man."

"In my eyes?"

"Yes. I thought of you when that man spoke to me. He spoke in your name, to protect you, yes, you, Hedwige, from men like me. He examined my papers, took my name. At this very moment, I'm listed among people who are watched, and it's my own fault."

Hedwige had unconsciously moved away to her bed. She stood there, motionless. Jean looked at her.

"I've shocked you," he said sadly.

"No, you haven't, Jean," she answered in a low voice, "but you've frightened me."

They were silent for a few minutes. Jean bent his head and seemed lost in thought. Hedwige did not move. Through the open window, the whispering of the great linden as it stirred in the breeze reached them, and the girl listened to the faint sound with a kind of gratitude. The sound was like a fountain's innocent babbling. She dared not tell Jean to leave her, but she would have liked him to vanish suddenly, taking his misfortune with him, for it did not affect her. He terrified her. For the first time, she noticed the size of his hands and tried to imagine all the evil actions they had perhaps committed: they had stolen, or struck or maybe killed someone. In Hedwige's mind, a fear of danger gave a peculiar likelihood to the harshest conjectures, but she was still too ignorant of life to guess the truth. Her knees shook. She sat down on the edge of her bed and drew the folds of her dressing gown over her breast.

"Jean," she said at last, "it's time you had some sleep."

He raised his head and looked at her. His glance was hardened by weariness.

"You are nothing but a little girl," he said slowly. Picking up his hat, he came close to her. "Listen, Hedwige, I've said nothing tonight of what I thought I would tell you. My heart failed me. Yet, I would have liked to tell someone the whole truth . . . someone like you . . . just to see. Someone pure. But it's a good thing that I didn't speak."

She turned her head away and blushed, furious at what she took for an insult.

"In spite of this," he continued, "I'd reproach myself if I didn't give you a piece of advice. I have your happiness in mind. Yes, it is about someone that you think about a great deal."

Hedwige gave an involuntary start.

"That very man," said Jean with a bitter smile. "I won't mention his name. That would be a kind of sacrilege, wouldn't it?"

"What do you mean, Jean? Have you seen him?"

"The day he came to this house, I had a glimpse of him through a window just as he was crossing the street. I slipped into the drawing room. . . ."

"Why?"

He hesitated, caught off his guard by this direct question.

"Why? Yes, it seems strange indeed. I never set foot in the drawing room when there are guests, but it interested me to observe . . . this person, to see him talking to this one and that. . . ."

"But why?"

He looked at her with parted lips, ill at ease suddenly. He pulled himself together, however.

"Let's put it down to psychological interest," he said in a slow, almost sneering tone, while he watched her childlike eyes with a kind of distrust, attempting to read in them what might be lurking at the back of her mind.

"I don't understand," murmured Hedwige.

Jean was seized with immense compassion. Indeed, she did not understand, she spoke truly. Whereas he lied. He hung his head.

"You're going to hate me," he said.

"I beg you to speak."

"My child," he said gently, "it would be better for you never to think about that young man again. No, don't ask me why! I cannot bear to read that question on your lips. But I know what I'm saying, Hedwige . . . my poor Hedwige."

She stood dazed and, all of a sudden, felt terrific anger

rising in her, an anger caused by fright, for she dreaded to know what Jean knew, and yet, in a quick, hoarse voice that she herself could not recognize, she cried out brusquely:

"I want to know!"

Jean shook his head. Then she grasped the lapels of his coat, as though she were about to tear them. He offered no resistance, did not budge.

"I can't tell you anything, unfortunately," he replied. "But if you're suffering, I'm suffering too, and in the same manner."

Hedwige's arms dropped. She was not interested in other people's sufferings. And how could Jean suffer in the same way she did? There was something alarming and obscure in everything he said. She looked silently at his grave, inscrutable face, his motionless eyes that either stared at her or avoided her glance, and was seized with a longing to strike his speechless, thin-lipped mouth, but dared not. For some time now, she had had a powerful sensation, one that she usually experienced faintly every time she met Jean on the stairs and playfully took his arm: a strange uneasiness, something vague and concealed, akin to disgust.

"Go away!" she whispered and drew away from him.

Chapter 6

Mme Vasseur sometimes thought of Félicie as being like a mouse that lived in a wall. That was the simile she used to describe the dressmaker when this person's name came up in the conversation. But this only happened on Fridays. For on a Friday, the dressmaker became a necessity, she really existed then, whereas no sooner had the Vasseurs' door closed on her than the old maid was swallowed up by the great, shapeless, tiresome mass of humanity, thought Mme Vasseur. Mme Vasseur even found it hard to believe that such an unobtrusive being could have worries, a few pleasures, clothes to put on in the morning and take off at night, a bed to rest in at night, letters to write and bills to pay, just as she did. To make things seem more probable, she preferred to stick to her favorite comparison and imagined Félicie in the shape of a mouse that was a little over life-sized. Does a mouse pay taxes? Does it go to the theater? Does it sometimes suffer from toothache? Mme Vasseur liked to establish this amusing parallel between an animal and a human being, and did so every Friday morning when she heard the dressmaker's timid ring at the door. She often burst into nervous laughter when she met the latter on the stairs because she so obviously looked like a mouse.

Félicie could make nothing of Mme Vasseur's merriment. She was quite unaware that her gray head, bent shoulders, and toddling walk might seem funny and connect her in anyone's mind with an animal that filled her with horror, but she blushed with shame and complained bitterly to Blanchonnet about the insolence of high society. Where were the days, she would ask the dummy, where were the days when Madame la Baronne used to come and converse with her dear Félicie and unburden her heart of its petty worries? Had Blanchonnet ever known a gentler, simpler woman, in spite of her title and great connections? Could Blanchonnet remember that a single unkind word had ever left those aristocratic lips? But the dummy kept a stupid, sinister silence. Whatever it knew was no one's business. And the dressmaker fancied that it stood even straighter and threw its bust forward.

On certain days, she hated Blanchonnet. At other times, she thought herself almost in love with it and, brushing the hollow breast with her lips, she would give the big black doll the kisses that no one had ever wanted. "Ah, my Blanchonnet!" she sighed. That was all she could say. Once, she let fly a kick that made it spin round and round, like a waltzer. She ill-treated or cajoled it, according to her mood. To her mind, in some inexplicable way, it represented all her disappointments, all her fears, all her desires, and all that remained to her of hope. At times, she transformed it into a superhuman being, at once better and worse than everyone else, open to flattery, capricious and resentful as a god; at others, she beat it like a dog and revenged herself on Blanchonnet for her own existence.

The other days of the week, she worked for various people who also furnished her with a dummy, but Mme Vasseur's stood out among its brothers and surpassed them all. It was handsomer, shinier, prouder, and it had seen Madame la Baronne die. So Friday was looked forward to with the delightful anxiety of love. One morning, she arrived a few minutes earlier than usual and slipped into the kitchen. Herbert, Monsieur's valet, was whistling softly as he polished his master's shoes. He was a big, bony, red-haired man with a sharp face and eyes that were hard to catch.

"Where's Berthe?" asked the dressmaker.

He nodded toward the pantry.

The cook sat before a bowl of black coffee, holding an envelope addressed to Madame to the light. She started as she saw the old maid enter and all but dropped the envelope into the coffee.

"You scared me," said Berthe. "No one ever hears you come in."

Félicie sank into a chair and pushed her black toque back slightly, so as to run her hand across her brow.

"It's happened again," she said. "I've had my dream."

"What, again!" cried the cook.

She laid her little, fat, red hands over her stomach and began to laugh.

"Herbert!" she called. "If Félicie hasn't gone and seen Madame la Baronne again!"

"Old lunatic!" exclaimed Herbert, without specifying to whom the epithet referred.

"Now don't laugh like that," said the dressmaker. "This time, I was so frightened that I couldn't get back to sleep. And this morning, suddenly, I had a feeling."

"It's been a good six weeks since you had one," said Berthe, swallowing down her coffee.

"We'll mark this one on the calendar with a cross," said Félicie. "You'll see, something is going to happen. She asked me for her blue cushion."

Herbert came in, his fist thrust into a shoe. He and the cook exchanged a wink while Félicie settled her pince-nez on her nose and, with stiff little gestures, made a cross on the calendar hanging on the wall.

"There," she said, turning with a look of mingled satisfaction and terror, as though she had just given fate an order. "Someone in this house is going to die."

"You're keen on that," said Berthe, sitting back in her chair and looking important. "You and the baroness bury somebody once a fortnight. Whom have you got your eye on this time?"

"Something dreadful is going to happen," said the dressmaker with a mysterious obstinacy.

Herbert dropped his shoe and sent it flying with a kick into the next room.

"Not in this house," he said with a sidelong glance. "These dirty dogs are much too lucky for that."

"And much too rich," added Berthe.

At these words, the dressmaker's little dark eyes began to sparkle behind her pince-nez, and she felt ungovernable hatred boil up inside her.

"Something is going to happen," she continued in a strangled voice.

The tone in which she said this created a kind of amazement. The dressmaker leaned against the wall and nodded, torn between delight in having an audience and fear of what she was about to say. For it seemed to her as though the words fell from her lips in spite of herself, and that she talked without being quite certain of what she had in mind. Suddenly, her heart thumped inside her black bodice and her pince-nez shook. Seized with a kind of dizziness, she thought that she saw the tiled kitchen floor wobble under her feet, like the bridge of a ship; at the same moment, a word rose to her lips, an immense word that resembled a long rolling of drums and a blood-red horizon. She said very distinctly, in a hollow voice:

"The revolution!"

And she ran off.

As she went through the pantry, she heard Berthe cry out:

"You call that something dreadful?"

She passed through the hall, as fast as her short legs allowed, and Mme Vasseur's comparison was doubtless never so apt as at the moment when the dressmaker walked up the first steps of the staircase, for the old maid bent double and ran noiselessly up, agile and wizened in her coal-black garments. She herself could not have said why she went so fast. It seemed as though she were running away, and indeed, perhaps she was running away, bearing off, like a treasure, the word she had just spoken. Fortunately, no one saw her in her excited condition. She reached the second story, opened the door of the room in which she worked, and, all out of breath, ran up to the dummy and struck it with her fist.

"Blanchonnet," she cried, "Blanchonnet, revolution!"

Then she looked around her, bewildered and a little frightened by what she had just done. Everything was tidy in the small room and the deepest silence prevailed in the house. The distant rumble of a cart on the boulevard was faintly heard, and closer, a bird call from the great linden in the courtyard. It was cool; a breeze trifled with a curtain at the open window. For two hundred years, the air and light had come into the room in the same fashion and revolutions had changed nothing there, but the dressmaker felt herself a new heart since she had spoken the magic syllables. Of all the rumors that went around the town, she remembered the word "revolution." She repeated it in a lower tone, then removed her toque, settled her pince-nez on her nose, and tried to imagine that Madame stood before her. Under such exceptional circumstances as the overthrow of a regime and in such excitement of mind, how should one behave? Félicie dared not believe that she would go so far as to strike Madame. She contented herself with striking Blanchonnet, who tottered. At that moment, the clock reminded Félicie that pending a general settling of scores, she might just as well braid Mlle Hedwige's pretentious jacket, as she had been told to.

So, five minutes later, she sewed that confounded black *soutache* on a navy-blue serge that was blinding her. She worked with an ardor that contained a good deal of ill temper, stabbing at the material with her needle as though she hoped to hurt it. Sometimes her narrow bosom heaved with a sigh of impatience and she cursed the fiendish caprices of an outmoded fashion, for all those vermiculations seemed hideous to her: on the sleeves and at the back, just below the waist, on the fronts too, here, there, and everywhere. Félicie shrugged her shoulders. Did Mlle Hedwige really think herself so pretty, to set her heart on such nonsensical trimmings? True, it was Madame who tricked her out like that. Everybody belowstairs knew that Hedwige accepted clothes that were given her to "finish," without a murmur. How many old frocks the dressmaker had let out, to give Hedwige breathing room! What a number of false pleats and false hems to smarten up the little provincial girl, and with what sinister results! Félicie took Blanchonnet to witness that no one could have worn her clothes worse. She got up suddenly, threw the ridiculous jacket over her shoulder, and walked up to the dummy, trying to swing her hips like Mlle Hedwige, but the skinniness of her body made the imitation most unconvincing. Shaking with silent laughter, the dressmaker stood on tiptoe to put the jacket on Blanchonnet.

"Anyway, *you* have a lovely figure," whispered Félicie, giving the dummy a pat.

Just as she said this, the door opened very gently and someone crept into the room. It was the concierge's little boy, the very one who had given the dummy the weird name of Blanchonnet. His round face smiled above the black apron that fell to his knees. He paused for an instant, cast large dark eyes around him as though he were looking for something, and then closed the door.

"Oh, it's you?" asked Félicie, in a slightly annoyed tone. "I give you fair warning that I have no time to waste today. What do you want?

"Mamma wants you to alter her bodice," he answered, circling around the dummy. "She says it won't take you half an hour and she'll pay you extra."

"Extra," muttered Félicie, tugging at the lapels of the jacket with a displeased expression. "Well, we'll see."

There was a silence during which Blanchonnet underwent a stiff examination. Félicie drew the *soutache* design on the jacket fronts with a piece of chalk and paid no attention to her visitor's absorbed air. All of a sudden, an excellent idea seemed to have struck the latter.

"Félicie!" he cried. "Supposing we pretend that Blanchonnet is Madame Pauque?"

"Ah! just you leave Blanchonnet alone," said Félicie, stretching out her arm in front of the dummy. "And you're keeping me from my work. Go away!"

"We could settle accounts!"

"Settle accounts with Blanchonnet! No indeed, you won't!"

"You never understand a thing, Félicie. Not with Blanchonnet: with Madame Pauque!"

Although this was a tempting suggestion, it roused Félicie's indignation as she foresaw that it would result in great danger for Blanchonnet. Turning her back on the dummy as if to protect him with her body, she ordered the little boy to go back to his mother.

"Mamma doesn't want me about," he said triumphantly. "She's sweeping. She told me to stay here."

Félicie refrained from remarking that old Ma Goral had plenty of nerve. She was afraid of the concierge, just as she was afraid of everybody else, and strange as it may seem, she was even afraid of this child of twelve who made a butt of her. So she kept a deep silence as she stuck pins into Mlle Hedwige's jacket. Several seconds went by, then the child disappeared behind a pile of hatboxes and Félicie could hear him moving about in a corner and humming. All of a sudden, he said very quietly:

"I may as well tell you, Félicie, that I'm going to kill you both, you and Madame Pauque."

Félicie loathed such jokes. She removed her pince-nez with a slightly shaky hand and answered that she would complain of him to his mother.

"Too late," said a voice from behind the hatboxes. "You two are crossing a desert infested by Arabs. There are at least two hundred of us behind this rock, and in a minute we're going to pot at you pitilessly.

But first, you must walk down this way a little and turn to the right. Then you'll be just within range of our guns. Do you get the idea, Félicie? Bang!"

"That's a silly game," said Félicie, starting involuntarily.

"Don't be scared," continued the voice. "You still have thirty more seconds to live. That's because you're walking slowly, because it's hot. Why, Madame Pauque has unfastened her bodice and she's fanning herself with her handkerchief. She's awfully sunburnt, is Madame Pauque! She looks like a Negress. Just a moment, I have a word to say to my hundred and ninety-nine comrades. I don't want any bad shots, or bungling, you know."

"Two hundred men against two women!" murmured Félicie, trying to laugh. "That's not a very nice way to behave."

"I can't help that," replied Marcel. "You deserve it. Just let me look at my chronometer. . . . You still have exactly ten seconds more to live. Would you like a glass of spirits, Félicie? One of my men will bring it to you. Oh no, it's too late and what good would it be? Come, be brave, my poor Félicie, it won't last long and perhaps you won't feel anything. One!"

"That's enough!" cried Félicie, stamping her heel on the floor.

"Two!" counted the voice.

"Marcel, I give you my word I'm going to slap you."

"You're jesting with death. Attention! Fire!"

The last word was drowned in a crash of tumbling hatboxes, and Marcel appeared with a white towel tied around his head and in his hand a long stick that he waved in Félicie's direction.

"Vengeance!" he cried, running at the old maid.

Félicie gave ground immediately and went to the door, protesting that she would tell Madame what took place in her house.

"I couldn't care less," said Marcel. "I'm going to finish off Madame Pauque, who is still breathing. She'll perish under torture."

Seizing Blanchonnet around the middle, he pretended to struggle with his victim for a moment, mimicking the tears and pleading of an expiring Mme. Pauque.

"No good begging for mercy," he cried. "You're in for it, old girl!"

In the flick of a wrist Blanchonnet was stretched out on the floor and Marcel took a several-bladed penknife from his pocket.

"Oh, no!" shrieked Mme Pauque in a high falsetto. "Why don't you torture Félicie instead of me, Monsieur Marcel?"

"Coward!" replied the young executioner. "We'll begin by removing one of your arms. Félicie's turn will come later," he added, "if, as I hope, she's still alive."

"Marcel!" cried the latter, from the door. "I'll tell Madame Vasseur. Leave Blanchonnet alone!"

But the child was not listening. Sticking out his tongue, he cut off an imaginary arm and threw it at Félicie's head, not without letting out a few roars.

"She's fainting," he said. "Quick, some coarse salt to sprinkle on her wound. That will bring her to."

Appalled, yet curious to discover how far the boy's cruelty would go, Félicie gave up all idea of obtaining a reprieve for Mme Pauque. In an almost inexplicable way, it seemed to her that the scene she had been witnessing for a little while gradually assumed the character of an almost supernatural truth. She became the child's accomplice and stood dumb and motionless, watched the strange agony of a woman she disliked and who, at that moment, embodied all the wrongs of an entire social system, in her eyes. A thirst for vengeance rose in her unfathomable little soul. She was overcome once more by the excitement she had felt a few moments before and began to murmur incoherently about triumph and hatred. She came a little closer and put on her pince-nez.

"Kill her," she said, under her breath.

"Not so fast," replied Marcel. "She's got to feel she's dying."

The old maid shivered. In the dummy's place, her imagination showed her a mutilated Mme Pauque in her black satin dress and blood spreading over it in wide crimson ribbons. Could it be that such a scene would ever take place in this town, that the revolution would enter this very room, with torches and pikes and bare arms? Instinctively, she bowed her shoulders and stuck her head out, like a frightened animal, and as though he read the dressmaker's thoughts the child leapt to his feet.

"We're going to guillotine her," he announced, placing his hobnailed boot on the dummy's hip. "Give me that chair, Félicie."

She brought the chair to the spot that Marcel showed her.

"Another one there!" he ordered.

She obeyed, carried away by the excitement of this horrible game, and placed a second chair in front of the first one. Then came a struggle between the executioner and his fainting victim and, almost at once, Blanchonnet was laid flat on its stomach, gasping and protesting in a feeble, broken voice.

"That's where her head is supposed to be," whispered the torturer, showing a gap between two rungs of one of the chairs. "The guillotine knife is here, Félicie." He added aloud, in a tone calculated to make an imaginary gallery of spectators tremble: "You shall be my assistant. This is the first time the guillotine has ever been used in the Sahara, but there's a beginning to everything. Come now, Félicie, I don't suppose you'll be scared at the sight of a little blood. Just tie up that hussy for me! I'll just make sure first that everything's in working order. The spring has been oiled. That's perfect. Be quiet, Madame Pauque. You deserve to die a hundred thousand times over and we're much too good to you. We ought to begin by the feet and cut you into slices, but that would be against all rules. Are you ready, Félicie? The crowd is getting restless."

He gave an imitation of an angry mob's confused muttering and booed in an undertone.

"That will do, my friends," he said with a flourish. "Do you think it's an easy job to cut off this wild woman's head? Just see how the hussy struggles! She tried to bite my assistant a moment ago, when she had a chance. There, take that and subside," he cried, dealing Mme Pauque a fresh kick. She began to howl dismally.

"Come on, come on, hurry up," continued Marcel, "this is getting painful. Félicie, just sit on her feet." As he spoke, he pretended to roll up the sleeves of his black apron and vigorously pressed a button in the vicinity of one of the chairs. He gave a kind of cluck, in imitation of a spring set in motion, and cried: "Ploof!" to signify that the head had rolled into the basket under the guillotine.

Félicie could not suppress a little cry of terror and moved away. At that instant, the boy turned to her, eyes shining, cheeks aglow.

"Now it's your turn!" he cried.

The dressmaker opened her lips, but terror gripped her throat and all she could do was to stutter incoherently. She felt as though she had just fallen into some diabolical trap and that, under cover of an unwholesome practical joke, this excited, noisy child was going to be the cause of her death. At the same time, the little room darkened around her. Instinctively, she held her hands out and backed. Her knees shook. She opened her mouth once more, but everything that was hunted, terrified in her soul was expressed by a very faint moan. Jumping aside, she took shelter behind a chair, when suddenly Marcel hoisted himself on Blanchonnet and, waving his arms, stood atop the dummy. A long-drawn-out cracking interrupted his gesticulations, then another cracking, this time short as a gunshot, and the child found himself seated on the floor next to Blanchonnet, whose stand had just snapped.

In the next few seconds neither Félicie nor Marcel could believe in the reality of what had happened.

"Blanchonnet!" said the dressmaker at last, blankly.

"Yes, Blanchonnet," said someone behind her.

It was Ulrique. She seemed taller than usual in the low-ceilinged room and more frightening too, more beautiful and more cruel with her hair streaming over her shoulders, her feet bare in red sandals. A white silk dressing gown covered her haughty bosom and long legs worthy of Diana. Her whole body exuded a perfume of amber and verbena, as though to shield her from the sorry odor of human beings. Her eyes big with boredom, she stared at some point above the dressmaker's head and murmured in a regal voice that contradicted the meaning of what she said:

"Félicie, I'm dumfounded."

"If Madame would allow me to explain!" cried Félicie, clasping little grayish hands.

"I don't care to know in the least," mumbled Ulrique. She turned her back on Félicie and went to the door, adding: "You woke me up. My mother will talk to you later."

Mme Vasseur appeared at that moment and asked what the matter was. Roused, like her daughter, by the racket on the floor above, she had thrown over her nightgown a mauve negligee whose sleeves floated around her, gesticulating. She had not troubled to fasten up her gray hair, and this added to the somewhat haggard expression that was natural to her, and turned her head this way and that, as though some invisible hand caught hold of her big, disapproving nose, to make a laughingstock of her. Not having listened to her daughter's explanations, she barked:

"I wish to know!"

Ulrique shrugged her shoulders.

"How dare you? How dare they?" demanded Mme Vasseur. "Félicie! Where's Félicie? And to begin with, why was I called here?"

None of the questions obtained a reply, but Félicie, hidden in a corner, sank onto a chair and melted into tears. Ulrique moved her chin to show Blanchonnet that lay at Mme Vasseur's very feet.

"Well," said the latter, "I still don't understand. Will somebody decide to speak?"

"It's not my fault," wailed the dressmaker, "I swear to Madame that I didn't do it."

Confronted by two dishevelled women, she lost her head and longed to throw herself at their feet, as she might have knelt before hostile divinities, but the fear of making them laugh prevented her, and she merely repeated that it was not she.

"I suppose Blanchonnet broke all by itself," said Ulrique, with a yawn.

At that moment, Marcel, who had hidden behind a piece of furniture at the first alarm, crept to the door and noiselessly disappeared.

"Blanchonnet!" exclaimed Mme Vasseur, understanding at last. "Well, I never! So that was the awful commotion I heard just now? Have you gone mad, Félicie? I'm sure she's mad," she added, turning to her daughter. "I've always thought so. Don't contradict me. Oh, dear!" she cried, remembering that she had left the water running in the bathroom.

And she left the room as abruptly as she had entered it. Ulrique followed her more deliberately.

Once alone, her ears still ringing with the sound of their quarrelsome voices, Félicie let a few minutes go by before she dared move. She watched the door anxiously, as though it might open to admit some evil spirit. Finally she left her chair and knelt by Blanchonnet, as she would have knelt by a corpse. The broken stump of wood protruding from the dummy seemed horrible to her. Her heart beat so fast that it hurt her and she clapped both hands to her breast, whispering an unfinished sentence: it was not her fault. She would have liked to explain this to Blanchonnet, but the dummy frightened her. It looked as though it had been struck by lightning and all she could do was to repeat its name with a mixture of terror and compassion, as if she feared it might answer her in a nightmarish voice.

Madame would probably dismiss her, deduct the price of the dummy from what she owed her. How much could a thing like a dummy cost? Ah, life was too cruel! Who would believe the dressmaker, if she accused that little devil of a Marcel? The concierge would be there, to stand up for her son. For a minute, Félicie buried her face in her hands and gave way to the extravagant ideas that whirled about in her brain. The dream she had had the night before came back to her then. Closing her eyes, she saw the baroness' face very clearly, not the kindly, lenient face she had known, but a face from beyond the grave, smiling evilly. And Félicie looked at it, in spite of herself, because there was something that fascinated her at the root of this terror, and because she wanted to know how the baroness would manage to appear to her now, without the assistance of Blanchonnet, who had been her vehicle.

"I must be losing my mind," she said, getting up suddenly. "I'd much better get on with my braid."

But her heart was not in her work and, try as she might, she sewed badly. Her shaking fingers sewed the braid crooked and soon she discovered that in her agitation she no longer followed the pattern, although she had it right there, under her eyes. Stimulated by fear, her mind galloped down sinister thoroughfares. Topped by a head, yet legless, Blanchonnet advanced toward her, opening greedy arms as if to catch her by the knees and make her fall. Félicie began to cry, not only over a phantasm that pursued her incessantly, but over her whole life, over a loveless youth, over the long, tedious years that ended in an absurd and sudden calamity. Had she been told, at sixteen, that what she had to expect at the end of her life was tears in a lonely room, was this little, dried-up old woman, bent and even a little humpbacked, a poor old creature who wept and wailed, she would have preferred death then and there. But at sixteen, she thought that someone might love her eventually, in spite of her sickly looks and the poverty in which her parents lived.

It gave her a kind of shock to look back upon the past, for she was not one to dwell on old memories; her chief concern was to hold out till the end of each week, and suddenly, with a flash of intuition that stirred her more deeply than everything else, she wondered, having successfully reached the end of countless weeks in the past, whether it was really worth while, if this constant struggle to keep from dying with hunger was not worse than death itself.

Chapter 7

Walking downstairs behind her mother, whose dreary gray locks floated over skinny shoulders, Ulrique suddenly decided to go away. In fact, she had been thinking of it for the last few days, but without knowing whether she wanted to or not, or why. And, all of a sudden, she realized that she could no longer bear to be with Mme Vasseur. The age and manias, even the attentions of this old lady, jarred on her nerves. She was not fond of her mother. She had suspected this for a long time: now, she was certain of it. Perhaps it was on account of Mme Vasseur's hideous dressing gown. It seemed to Ulrique that, for the first time in her life, she really noticed the ugliness of that great haggard profile, that turkey neck, that lank body wriggling about futilely in a dowdy wrapper, a wrapper fit for a concierge, she thought. "I'd cross half of Europe," she said to herself, "to avoid meeting that wrapper."

She went to the bathroom and slipped into tepid water, as though it were a bed. Her contented glance wandered from her breast to her hips, followed the shape of her long legs. How few had seen that magnificent body! Smiling, she recalled hopes that she had not quite discouraged till the very last minute, attentions received and at first accepted, to be scorned later, the ludicrous rage of her victims, the coarseness of men. . . .

The coarseness of men was a theme to which her mind had constantly reverted, since her atrocious bridal night. Four years of marriage had not been enough to wipe away the shame and ridicule of being delivered, through her mother's agency, to a hairy little man whose advances filled her with horror. To have been the instrument of that fool's pleasure seemed an insult that would rankle in her as long as her husband lived. It was not enough to refuse to live with him, to lead him to think that she was unfaithful to him; she wanted more, she found him too patient, too resigned. She had a suspicion, at times, that he no longer desired her much and the idea tortured her. As to Mme Vasseur, Ulrique punished her continually for having made such an unfortunate choice, heaped contempt on her, drew tears that the poor woman shed copiously over the make-up that coated her faded cheeks. Too vain and too adroit to complain of her husband, she hinted that Mme Vasseur was in love with him and had forced him on her daughter in order to have him near, in her house.

"Oh!" cried Mme Vasseur, once she had understood, which was not always the case.

"What's surprising about that?" asked Ulrique. "It happens so often. . . ."

She forgave Raoul his crass foolishness, his bogus good manners, his platitudes, and even his cupidity; she could not excuse his ugliness and short legs, his mustache and a skin that went with sandy hair, or a bodily odor that cologne did not remove. Of course, she had found compensation in other quarters, but less often than she led her both scandalized and admiring mother to believe. From boredom and also from disgust, she discouraged men who would have satisfied a more sensual woman. This quest for perfect beauty was really no more than a disguised frigidity, but Ulrique would never have accepted such a simple explanation and preferred to think herself the victim of her artistic sense, as she clumsily expressed it.

"They're so ugly, so common," she would say to her friend Arlette, "particularly when . . . well . . ."

Arlette turned a profile, which was that of a young porker crowned with a golden fringe, toward Ulrique.

"My dear Ulrique," she said, "all you have to do, at certain moments, is to close your eyes. You're too fastidious. I've been dealing in antiques for the last five years and am beginning to realize that every work of art is partly faked. This doesn't prevent there being good bits, on the whole. But you refuse everything because you're suspicious of the spurious parts. You're wrong there. You want something completely genuine. It doesn't exist."

"Not here at least, in this dreary town."

Arlette shrugged her shoulders and laughed.

"Now you're going to talk about those trips of yours. In my case, it's much simpler: I simply telephone, just like that."

She would then recount her latest adventure. Ulrique made a face.

"That little Gérard? With those prominent eyes . . ."

"Popeyes," replied Arlette. "Why don't you say popeyes and spoil him for me completely? To begin with, his eyes are like those in a portrait by Clouet, and I just adore that. And then, you haven't seen him as I have. . . ."

Followed a description in an exclamatory style that made Ulrique raise her eyebrows, for she severely judged her friend the antique dealer's vulgarity, and pretended not to listen, although she heard every word, and most distinctly. Gérard's person was described with passionate greed, and for a few minutes, so aptly did the garrulous Arlette choose her words, it seemed as though the youth were present in the back shop where this smutty conversation took place, and that he stood there, among half-spurious bits of furniture, fans, and beribboned portraits.

"Congratulations," said Ulrique, at last. "You have a very good time, I see."

"It remains with you to find out that I haven't exaggerated in the least. Young Gérard admires you enormously, but he's scared of you. Would you like me to fix up something?"

"Have you gone mad, by any chance? I don't need anyone yet to fix up things for me."

"My dear," said Arlette, stung to the quick, "you put on fewer airs when I found young Dolange for you."

"Gaston Dolange!" cried Ulrique. "I wouldn't have him for anything in the world. I had someone else in mind that I thought he might suit."

Sly puss, thought Arlette.

"And he's hideous, anyway," added Ulrique.

"Hideous, that may be, but everyone is crazy about him."

And so these two idiots conversed. Arlette's shop was situated on one of the town's most elegant quays and patronized by customers who were rich, wary, and guileless, all in one. Smart women cast distant glances at valuable curios and a middle-aged dealer whose every wrinkle grinned at them. At such times, Ulrique would hide behind a calamander screen, at the back of the shop, because she was ashamed of her friend Arlette, although she appreciated her freedom of speech added to an extraordinary skill in the art of dissimulation. Ulrique also secretly envied her a life filled with intrigues and excesses. How common she is! she thought as she listened to tales that always ended in the same manner. And once she was home, she turned them over in her mind, adorning and correcting Arlette's descriptions in such a way as to change these wretched carnal adventures into an Arabian Night.

Once or twice only had she taken advantage of what Arlette chastely called her advice; this meant that at the close of an afternoon, she found herself in some unknown person's flat, with the antique dealer and one or two young men whose looks were far too good for them to have been present by chance, so good that even the icy Ulrique felt a little excited. Their voices had vulgar intonations, to be sure, and they held a cup as they would a bowl, but their smile excused everything. Ulrique eluded them for several weeks, then consented to be led into temptation, even though, at the last moment, she recovered her self-control.

In Mme Vasseur's drawing room one met only gentlemen of a wretched physical aspect, disfigured by high living or office work. Ulrique did not even notice them. What is called a man of the world represented, in her imagination, something bewhiskered and funereal that she assiduously avoided. However, she was far too young, too beautiful, and too feminine to accept her lovers from the hands of a procuress. Rather than resort to Arlette's good offices, she preferred to wall herself up in loneliness, as though it were a palace, and obtain from music a little of the somber enjoyment she loved.

As she soaped her body that morning, she wondered when she would meet the ideal being to whom she sometimes talked in secret. She gave him tastes like her own and a face like that of the great curly-locked Hermes who adorned a niche on a landing of the grand staircase. She would have been very much surprised to be told that those were the dreams of a little girl and that she was unduly prolonging her childhood. She came to envying her cousin, for she at least could tell herself that her ideal existed in the flesh, eating and drinking. Now, it was precisely on Hedwige's account, and because she foresaw some great misfortune, that she wanted to go away, but she would never have admitted it, even to herself.

Something took place that afternoon that was never mentioned, for it seemed incredible and even the actors in this little drama wondered, for a long time, whether they had not dreamt it. With a little thought, both of them would have realized that the thing had to happen, but they were incapable of establishing a link between several ideas and of discerning the necessity of certain actions. So, at about three in the afternoon, it happened that the dressmaker passed Ulrique on the grand staircase and right there, under the eyes of Hermes, without any apparent reason and no provocation, slapped her.

The direct cause of this gesture was a glass of brandy which the cook and manservant had just persuaded Félicie to swallow. The old maid never drank anything but wine and water and, in itself, a small glass of spirits was sufficient to make her gray head swim. True, it had taken many a patient effort to convince Félicie that a thimbleful of that nice liqueur could only be good for her. At first she had hesitated, smelling a rat. To begin with, that brandy came out of Monsieur's cellar. Wasn't it stealing, to drink it? And then, Herbert was overinsistent and the sly fellow's pleasantness made Félicie uneasy. Since the beginning of the meal, he had in fact devoted all his attentions to the dressmaker, who thought him a rather fine-looking man, and all of a sudden he began to talk about the future "general social upheaval." Now, no matter how many mental reservations could be made concerning Herbert's morality, it had to be admitted that when he talked about the general social upheaval, he talked well. He did not get excited; quite the contrary: the more terrible the things he said, the calmer he grew. His information came from reliable sources and he delivered it in a confidential, measured tone, without unnecessary gestures. Long red lashes veiled his sea-green eyes, his hand played carelessly with a knife, his lips scarcely moved, and the words in which he settled everyone's score seemed to force their way out grudgingly. Everyone's score: first that of ministers of state, then came certain questionable generals, the clergy in a body, the rich, Mme Vasseur, Mme Pauque, Ulrique. He knew what he was saying, did Herbert. He was sorry that there would have to be excesses, for he was an easygoing fellow, but like a prophet of old and with a slightly different vocabulary, he announced to his small audience that soon everything was going to bust.

Félicie liked this highly alarming speech. She was frightened, but delightfully so, and when Herbert proposed that they should drink to the revolution, an icy little shiver seemed to run down the dressmaker's spine.

Scarcely had she swallowed her brandy than she felt a voluptuous warmth throughout her little body, an agreeable emptiness in her head. She began to laugh, without quite knowing why. Herbert exchanged a wink with the cook and Félicie vaguely realized that they were making fun of her, but did not resent it. Her pince-nez awry, she waved her hand lightheartedly, grinning broadly at her tablemates.

However, two o'clock struck and yards of *soutache* waited for the dressmaker to turn into elegant vermiculations. So she got up and went to the door. No sooner had she taken a few steps than she felt that she was walking too straight, and that it would look more natural and be easier to walk a little less straight. This she at once put into practice, to Herbert and Berthe's great merriment, and their shouts of laughter followed her to the grand staircase.

On reaching it, she threw herself at the banister, grasped it in both hands, and, once she was quite sure that the house would budge no longer, walked up very slowly, saying "Up you go!" each time she raised her foot. She went up half of the first flight in this fashion and found herself at last facing the big curly-haired Hermes that she had never dared look at squarely, for it should be said that he was stark naked. But that day, Félicie felt herself a new woman and boldly settled her pince-nez to examine this work of art. She thought it rather ugly and burst into scornful laughter in front of this shameless man who, strangely enough, held a small child on his arm.

That was the moment when Ulrique passed between the Greek god and the dressmaker, and her silent, haughty step was like that of a statue in motion. Her still glance looked beyond the white walls toward some entrancing spot, and she probably did not see the little creature clinging to the banister, dressed all in black. And, all of a sudden, the unaccountable thing happened: Félicie raised a flabby hand and struck Ulrique on the cheek.

The two women drew apart simultaneously, as though some deadly engine had just exploded at their feet. Ulrique looked down and stared at the dressmaker, but did not take in what had happened. On one hand, she felt something on her cheek, on the other was that absurd Félicie looking at her with a horrified expression, but what connection could there be between these two facts? She hesitated, smoothed her eyebrows with her fingertips, and went on her way, without saying a word.

Félicie stayed where she was for several minutes, clinging to the banister like a bat that could not take flight. She puffed, nodding her head, muttering disjointed bits of sentences that sounded at times like a prayer and at others like apologies. There was a somewhat lengthy pause before she dared move, then she peeped around her and, seeing nothing, grew bolder and zigzagged up to the top story.

Chapter 8

HEDWIGE HAD A PAINFUL RECOLLECTION of her conversation with Jean and hoped never to see him again, so much had his remarks and appearance frightened her. She could not succeed in recognizing her former friend under this new aspect. He looked like a hunted animal, and this upset her more than anything else. So she learned with a kind of relief that he was preparing to take a rather long journey, but Mme Pauque, who brought Hedwige this piece of good news, was extremely circumspect and gave very few details, although she had the air of someone who knew far more than she said; it should be added, however, that this was Mme Pauque's habitual expression.

"Why Naples?" asked Hedwige.

"My child," answered Mme Pauque, clasping hands sparkling with amethysts, "why not Naples? He has business there."

"It's a long way off."

Mme Pauque lowered her eyelids, raised her chin slightly, half smiling. "That's just it," she murmured.

"How stupid I am!" cried Hedwige. "Aunt Emma is sending him there to look up things about our family tree."

At that moment, Mme Pauque smiled even more subtly and more knowingly than she had a short time before, and left the room.

Hedwige was not mistaken, but she had small merit in guessing the reason for a journey that was the topic of Mme Vasseur's conversation several times a year. For a long time, in fact, the old lady had talked about the Royal Library in Naples as though it were a kind of family burial vault where illustrious great-great-uncles slept side by side with what she invariably termed dusty records. She was sure that enough could be found in Naples to justify her claims to what was, according to her point of view, an exceptionally honorable ancestry. For she was secretly worried about what Ulrique thought of her and the plebeian blood that perhaps flowed in her veins. Sometimes, she woke up at dawn and turned such matters over in her head. "Perhaps," she said to herself, "Grandmother Frivolini didn't belong to a very good family, after all." And she added with almost touching humility in such a proud woman: "Oh dear, it's just possible that I'm a tiny bit common." That was why she wondered, as she looked at her husband sleeping innocently at her side, how Ulrique could be so distinguished. Poor Bernard, she thought, you don't look a thoroughbred, like Georges Attachère. How elegant he was! Even his contempt took the form of politeness. What would that exquisite person have thought of you? A loud and vulgar snore was the usual answer to this unfair question.

Mme Vasseur had talked frankly to Jean more than once about a matter she had so much to heart. She could tell that Jean had a certain contempt for her, but he could not alter the fact that he and she were second cousins; what was more, he owed it to her that he lived comfortably in her house, free to come and go as he pleased, without having to account to anyone for a rather mysterious life. For this reason, she considered it her right to force her way into his room and propose that he should undertake genealogical researches which he considered completely useless. "A tree," repeated Mme Vasseur, "we must have a family tree. Jean, you would do that sort of thing to perfection." He looked at her then, with great dark eyes where boredom burnt like a flame.

"My dear," he said finally, shuffling his papers, "I have a book to finish."

"Oh, you've been finishing it for the last ten years! Lay it aside for a while. You're too serious-minded. You should have a holiday. Take this little trip to Naples. Monsieur Vasseur will treat you to it."

Jean expected the last sentence with scarcely concealed pleasure, for it allowed him to refuse the whim of a woman who did not always show much delicacy in her dealings with him and sometimes mentioned money, a subject he loathed.

"I'm sorry," he said, with feigned sadness.

One evening, however, he went to Mme Vasseur and briefly told her that he accepted her offer. He talked fast, like a man in a great hurry, and although he seemed very calm, a woman who was more observant than Mme Vasseur would have realized that he was controlling his feelings, but she was all joy at seeing her little scheme prosper and did not notice her cousin's excessive pallor.

"I've reached a point in my studies," he explained, "where it's necessary for me to take this journey. I'll have to go several times to the Naples museum to complete my iconography of St. Sebastian."

"Of course," said Mme Vasseur, without the least idea of what he meant and her thoughts centered on her family tree.

He added in a tone that harbored a great deal of resentment:

"As I'm too poor to afford this trip, I'll be glad to undertake the work you mentioned. My expenses . . ."

She cut him short by falling on his neck.

He left early next morning, without making a sound, without disturbing anyone, and his only luggage was a small black trunk, a pauper's trunk.

Ulrique left a little later, but with less simplicity: from the crack of dawn, she scolded her mother, who fussed around the pigskin suitcases and shagreen dressing-bags, mixing up bottles, putting away the things that Ulrique planned to take with her. Already, Mme Vasseur mourned for her daughter and missed her overbearing ways before she had left the house.

"Do give me your address at least," she wailed.

But Ulrique was inflexible on that point.

"You can write to me care of Arlette," she muttered.

Her father vainly added his pleadings to Mme Vasseur's, for although he was afraid of his daughter, he also loved her blindly, tenderly, and returned to his room to hide his grief when he heard the front door close on the lovely, ungrateful Ulrique. Raoul, on the contrary, showed a beaming face. As for Hedwige, who thought herself forgotten, as her cousin had not said good-by to her, she went off to devour this new sorrow in the solitude of a little sitting room.

Curled up in a big tapestry armchair, she drew the muslin curtain aside from the windowpanes and let her eyes wander over a street that was almost always deserted and lined with ancient, blackened houses. This somewhat melancholy view soothed her; she had almost come to like a sidewalk where no one ever went by, tall façades sullied by age and that seemed only to harbor boredom or gloomy domestic joys.

She started suddenly. A man standing motionless across the street from the Vasseurs' house looked up at her. There he stood, on the sidewalk, motionless. She moved quickly away from the window, but almost at once this seemed ridiculous to her. Why should that man be looking at her? He probably did not even see her. She began to watch him, through the curtain. He smoked a cigarette and occasionally turned his head this way and that, as though he were expecting someone, then he took a few steps in front of the house, threw away his cigarette, and thrust his hands into his pockets with the airy expression of a man who has absolutely nothing to do, but his eyes never left the house and, quite obviously, he was on the lookout for something, or someone. He was neither well nor badly dressed, in dark blue. Of middle height, he wore a small short mustache that underlined a thick mouth, the color of raw meat. Apart from that, he seemed most commonplace: nothing in his appearance distinguished him from hundreds of other strolling pedestrians whose faces are at once forgotten. But Hedwige looked at the man for several minutes and did not forget him.

PART TWO

Chapter I

ONCE A YEAR, at the first signs of spring, the whole house fell into Mme Pauque's hands. Reserved and almost timid until then, she turned energetic and aggressive, like a machine that never ceased revolving, threshing, and crushing. She was seized with a kind of springtime disorder and could be met in passages, her mouth full of pins, her arms full of paper, going about her mission with an unshakable faith in the virtues of camphor and naphthalene.

She carried everything before her, went in and out as she pleased with a freedom that belongs only to death itself. Plunging long, thin hands into the furthermost parts of wardrobes, she brought out the garments on which she was about to exert her ardor; on rugs overspread with paper, she laid out dresses, wraps, and overcoats, lifeless victims that she prepared for burial, according to a sumptuous ceremony. With masterly precision, she dropped into folds of serge the mystical pinch of powder that preserved the material from corruption. This observance was performed in a deep silence, broken only by the faint tinkling of the chains that decked Mme Pauque's breast, and from time to time by a murmur of satisfaction heralding the salvation of a suit or coat. Sometimes, she knelt by clothes that retained something human in their attitudes, and touched their shoulders, as much as to reassure them, or with a slyly pious air slipped a few moth balls into their pockets, and a smell of naphthalene floated about her person and clung to it. Next, sleeves were folded one over the other for a long summer sleep, and great brown paper bags swallowed up strange corpses, laid away in the darkness of cupboards to await the promised resurrection.

What interested Mme Pauque most in the suits and dresses that she laid away with such ceremony was their resemblance to people who, through long usage, had given them something of their personality, and she always felt slightly moved, in a curious but not unpleasant manner, to see these mysterious doubles lying before her, delivered into her hands: M. Vasseur's double, and his wife's double, Ulrique's double, Raoul's double; Jean's double, the humblest one of all; little Hedwige's double too; and last, more disturbing than any other, Mme Pauque's double, with its black laces, jet-spangled dresses, crape and all its solemn fal-lals.

It was not easy to discover what took place in Mme Pauque's mind, nor what kind of happiness she found in accomplishing her task, but it sometimes happened, when she felt sure of being completely alone, that sentences, punctuated by lengthy sighs, escaped her pale lips. She talked to the doubles. In a soft low voice that grew louder suddenly before dropping to an almost unintelligible whisper, she foretold their fate.

"Poor thing!" she said, sprinkling pinches of camphor over M. Vasseur's suit. "Too short for his weight, too short. That's bad. Dangerous."

Looking at a pearl-gray dress crazily strewn with white roses, she nodded yes, then shook her head to mean no, as though in reply to questions asked by an inner voice. "Emma!" she murmured simply, in a reproachful voice, for it was Mme Vasseur's evening dress.

With her smooth face, black hair, and upright figure, she looked young and old at the same time, and felt herself to be a little mysterious, not only in other people's eyes, but in her own: although she was beautiful, gentle, and good according to the normal way of judging, she was not attractive to anyone.

She thought vaguely about all this in the hanging closet next to Ulrique's room and sprinkled naphthalene over the black velvet cape that her niece sometimes wore to the theater. Ulrique had not written for two weeks. A few hastily scribbled words on a postcard had informed the Vasseurs (and before them, Mme Goral, the cook, manservant, and Félicie) that the temperature was delightful at Nice. That was all. Mme Pauque disapproved of her niece's journey, was pessimistic about her long silence, but said nothing about it, merely holding her tongue with a kind of sinister eloquence when Mme Vasseur asked her why Ulrique did not write. No one knew how to be silent like Mme Pauque, nor in a more alarming manner. She excelled at saying nothing and kept a sphinxlike stillness where an exclamation, a sigh, or merely a nod was expected of her. Such, at that moment, was her attitude before the orgulous velvet cape spreading at her feet, which she considered at great length; and, without removing her eyes from the wrap, she began rubbing her hands together.

A clock chimed and interrupted a meditation that absorbed Mme Pauque to the point of making her start when she heard the high-pitched stroke tell the hour. She grew pink, as though she had been caught in some misdemeanor and hastily slipped the cape into its paper coffin before putting it away with dresses belonging to Hedwige and Mme Vasseur.

This task completed, she remembered Jean; she thought less often of him than about other members of the family, although he also interested her, and decided on the spot to go up to his room and take his clothes the blessings of camphor. An opportunity to enter his room almost never offered, and his journey to Naples happened in the nick of time: she would not have to struggle with this touchy man, in order to be trusted with his winter clothes. So she walked up to the top story and boldly opened the door.

A little shiver of pleasure ran down her spine when she found herself in the small room that she had not seen since her early youth, and she looked around her with eyes that could not glut her curiosity. Yet, the room was extremely commonplace: it had an iron bedstead and a curtainless window, and looked like a servant's room; the deal table and straw-bottomed chair confirmed this impression. A maid's room or a cell, thought Mme Pauque. Yes, a monk's cell.

This seemed all the truer to her since she had never seen a monk's cell, but she fancied that the same simple furnishings, the same severity would be found there, and this austere setting was, to her mind, the reflection of a personality all the more attractive for its weirdness. For, when all was said and done, who could pride themselves on knowing Jean? His extreme reserve, his taste, no, his passion for secrecy, shielded him from the most obstinate curiosity, and when one had said that he was serious-minded, had not everything been said?

She walked about the room a little, casting her eyes around her with a kind of self-contained eagerness. In a corner stood the pitch-pine wardrobe containing the clothes she would presently bury in pharmaceutical aromatics, and she was going toward that cupboard when her eye was caught by two photographs fastened to the wall with drawing pins, just postcards and, to speak truthfully, very clumsily colored.

The first represented a religious scene, the Last Judgment, no doubt, for a crowd of naked men and women could be seen, showing terror by hiding their faces, or gesticulating, while bat-winged devils were already bustling around them. Mme Pauque read Signorelli's name at the foot of the postcard and thought the work a proof of the faultiness of bygone artists, who did not know how to draw correctly, and also of their morbid, superstitious minds. Could anyone have painted an uglier, more unpleasing scene, or one expressed in a more childish fashion? And then, all these nude bodies . . . She wondered whether Jean were not a trifle fanatical.

The second photograph seemed less forbidding, although extremely mysterious. It showed a young man who bent one knee and assumed the attitude of an archer; however, to her astonishment, he did not hold a bow, but the intentness of a warrior determined not to miss the mark could be read in his sullen face. Long curly hair framed his face. Under this picture was the name of Michelangelo, followed by that of St. Sebastian.

"How quaint," said Mme Pauque, under her breath.

She did not imagine that St. Sebastian looked like that. Was he not, as a rule, changed into a living pincushion, long arrows thrust into his breast and shoulders? Perhaps the artist had made a mistake. If she had been Jean, she would have chosen something more accurate, but she remembered that he contemplated writing a book about artistic reproductions of St. Sebastian, so perhaps this document merely presented the interest of an erroneous conception. Really, it invited laughter.

"It's a scream!" she murmured.

And freely giving vent to subdued gaiety, she threw her head back and gave a faint chuckle. That absurd Jean! she thought, her eyes moist.

Recovering her composure, she opened the wardrobe and took out an overcoat that made her shake her head, for it was threadbare, and a blue serge suit, shiny with wear. Not without a little uneasiness, Mme Pauque unhooked these clothes and spread them on the bed. For all sorts of reasons, she disliked poverty, and what she mentally called old togs reminded her of nothing else. The suit seemed particularly shabby. The overcoat obviously belonged to a man who was a failure, not a beggar, certainly, but a gentleman who accepted financial assistance. One could feel it. . . . And the overthin overcoat she had seen formerly, when the material was still good, on M. Vasseur's back; there was something humble and ashamed about it at present that embarrassed her. However, she dropped a few camphor balls into the pockets with a merciful hand and was about to open the paper bag that she had spread on the table when a sound of voices took her to the window.

Mme Goral, the concierge, was holding forth: her rough voice, deep and bellowing, interrupted a man as he persistently repeated a sentence the words of which were lost in space and did not reach Mme Pauque's ear. The latter softly opened the window and cast a sidelong glance into the courtyard, from under her long eyelids.

What she saw made her start from astonishment.

Two men stood before the concierge, and Mme Pauque recognized one of them as the baker who catered to the family; the other was obviously his son: both had the same golden hair, the same rather sly face that seemed powdered over with flour, but while the father was broad-shouldered and very thick in the waist, the son, whom Mme Pauque had never seen, looked almost a lad, in spite of his light gray linen trousers and the cheeky way he looked Mme Goral up and down.

Mme Pauque instinctively raised one hand and placed it on her breast as she leaned out slightly, in order to hear more distinctly.

"But I'm telling you that we just want to speak to him," repeated the young man, in a voice that grew loud and peremptory.

"For the twentieth time, I'm telling you he's away," growled Mme Goral. "Would you like me to call a policeman . . . ?"

At these words, Mme Pauque closed the window abruptly. She did not like people to make a noise in the courtyard, particularly tradesmen, persons from the lower classes, with their quarrelsome voices. It seemed too much like a scandal, like what was most horrible in her eyes. Emotion made her pant very slightly. ". . . He's away . . ." They were referring to Jean, but what could that mean? Why did the baker and his son wish to speak to Jean? What connection could there be between the scholarly, reserved, quiet Jean and these two rough, noisy men? Her big, worried eye rested on the St. Sebastian that had made her laugh, a moment before, but she no longer laughed. At present, she did not even see the avenging archer who seemed to be aiming at her.

Outside, the noise died down. There was a last bark

from the concierge and Mme Pauque thought that she caught the word "police," then, suddenly, all was silence, a silence that restored peace to her troubled heart. Venturing one more glance from the window, she gave a sigh: the courtyard was empty. One might have thought that nothing had taken place there, and Mme Pauque hoped that no one would ever mention that inexplicable scene to her, for she was the kind that preferred not to know.

With careful hands, she folded clothes that lay on the bed, their sleeves outstretched like the arms of victims; she ran her fingers over the lapels of the suit and overcoat; repeating this gesture several times, it seemed to reassure her.

"It was nothing," she murmured, "nothing at all."

When she was about to leave the room, her work finished, she cast a long inquiring look around her and went out noiselessly, after locking the door.

Chapter 2

A FEW DAYS AFTER, Hedwige and Mme Vasseur promenaded on the city mall, under plane trees whose first shoots formed a kind of network over the pale blue sky. The two women paused only when they reached the end of the walk to retrace their steps, engaged in a murmur of small talk that dispensed them from dealing with a more serious topic. Unfortunately, this game could not be prolonged beyond certain limits, which they very well knew; that was perhaps why Hedwige looked extremely pale and Mme Vasseur pulled at her gloves and made sure that her keys lay at the bottom of her handbag.

We're going home in five minutes, thought Mme Vasseur. She will have had an airing, maybe she'll be able to eat a little dinner. I hope she isn't going to begin talking to me all over again about that M. Dolange before we get back to the house. Once we're home, I can always get away, go up to the third floor to give Félicie directions, or go down to the kitchen where everything is always at sixes and sevens. But here . . . Oh! Ulrique, how could you be so cowardly as to go off, leaving me with this nuisance on my hands! No, not cowardly. Ulrique isn't a coward, but what a pity it is she doesn't come back! She's the only one who knows how to talk to the child. . . .

If, thought Hedwige, we pass the third tree in this

row, and if, at that instant, my aunt doesn't open her bag, but looks at me in silence, as she sometimes does, that will mean I'll see M. Dolange before the end of the month.

"I never come here," said Mme Vasseur aloud, "without remembering a trip I took to Naples, in 1902, the year Ulrique was born. It's very strange. I don't know why I always think about it here. There was a hideous bearded beggar who winked at me."

She's saying the first thing that enters her head, thought Hedwige, and we've passed the tree.

"Bernard," continued Mme Vasseur, "wanted to give him something. He's so guileless. . . . But our guide had explained that all the beggars in Naples had wads of banknotes sewn into their mattresses. I had a good laugh as I translated the guide's explanations, for, as you can imagine, Bernard hadn't understood a word; he doesn't know Italian; the guide and I chatted together in that tongue. The guide was such a decent sort, with such a straightforward expression. . . . He told me all about the Camorra's evil deeds. Such tales! They've all dropped out of my mind, but were really astounding. Wait a minute! There was one about a lawyer. No, it was about a doctor. Anyway, it gave me the shudders as I listened to the guide. I made Bernard give him an unusually large *mancia*. Bernard wanted to haggle with the man. He's a little close-fisted at times, is Bernard, he doesn't quite know how to behave in a lordly manner. . . ."

How happy she is, although she doesn't know it, thought Hedwige. She can sleep at night.

"The guide took the *mancia* with a wonderful flourish," continued Mme Vasseur. (She repeated the gesture with a grand sweep of her arm that almost made

Hedwige smile.) "And he said, looking me straight in the eye: 'Signora, it's not so much the *mancia*' (A *mancia,* child, is a tip), 'it's not so much the *mancia* that pleases me, although it will allow me to buy a little white bread for Mamma and some tobacco for my poor Nonno who worked so hard when he was young, no, it's the truly exquisite conversation—*veramente squisita*—that I have had with the Signora Contessa.' For I had forgotten to tell you that he called me Signora Contessa. Oh! no doubt there was a suspicion of flattery in all this, but still, he knew whom he was talking to. Fancy, Hedwige, he absolutely insisted on kissing my hand. Of course Bernard thought this ridiculous, but the guide, with a sort of impetuousness, seized the tips of my fingers and quickly carried them to his lips. Such grace in a man of the people . . . He went part of the way with us and just before we reached our hotel, he made us a low bow and said to me that if ever the Signora heard anyone remark that people in Naples were not obliging, nor above all honest, she should be good enough to remember the guide who had shown her over the aquarium and the Church of San Giovanni and that if, by some unlucky chance, some rogue took advantage of her trustingness—for dishonest people are to be found everywhere—would the Signora kindly recall the face of this very guide, her obedient servant, and his name: Sisto Bellini, for he had friends without number at the *Questura,* among the police, and he would act, Signora, he would act! Whereupon, with another bow, deeper and even more respectful than the first, off he went, at an easy pace, stroking his long mustache. . . ."

She sighed.

"And what happened next, Aunt Emma?" asked

Hedwige mechanically, for she knew the story by heart.

"What happened next, my child, was far less brilliant. We returned to the hotel, and in the hall I gave a scream: 'Bernard, my bag!' Do you know what was left of my bag? Its straps hanging over my arm. The bag itself had been cut away, oh, with such skill! I almost fainted. For with it I lost a thousand-lire banknote, a gold pencil, a vanity case, also gold, five twenty-franc pieces, a wonderful miniature of Monsieur Georges Attachère, and my keys. I was given a chair, offered a glass of water, and at that moment gave another scream. Without being able to utter a word, I showed your uncle my right hand: its glove had gone, also every one of its rings: the ruby my mother left me, the diamond Bernard gave me when we were married, the little cameo with a head of Caligula—was it Caligula or Demosthenes? Be it as it may, I fainted dead away."

"And when you came to," said Hedwige, hoping to shorten the narrative, "you found yourself in the presence of a man in uniform."

"A lieutenant of the police militia," specified Mme Vasseur, "a magnificent figure of a man," she continued with all the innocence of a dotard. "He was writing something down in a notebook and nodding as he pretended to listen to Bernard. Now Bernard proved himself hopelessly incompetent during the whole business. He wanted to have our guide arrested at all costs, and said over and over again: 'Someone must be sent to the man's home. His name is Sisto Bellini. His house must be searched.' Each time he mentioned Sisto Bellini's name, I could see the manager, concierge, and lieutenant start and glance this way and that. 'Bernard, you're too foolish!' I cried."

When I'm old, thought Hedwige, perhaps I'll tell such stories. But I would never have spoken like that to Gaston Dolange. . . .

For the hundredth time, she tried to imagine what her life with Gaston Dolange could be like, and lost herself in a melancholy and delicious meditation.

"My idea was also to look for our guide," continued Mme Vasseur, "not to arrest him, *Dio!* but to ask his advice. Hadn't he told me himself to call on him in case of need? One could have sworn that the man, on account of some instinctive attraction to me, had had something in the nature of a foreboding. The captain of the police militia hesitated a bit and began to talk Neapolitan to the manager. Finally, it was decided to send a *carabiniere* to Sisto Bellini's house. An hour later . . . Are you listening, Hedwige?"

"Yes, Aunt Emma. An hour later . . ."

"An hour later, I heard a knock at the door of my room. It was not our guide, but the officer we had seen a short time before. *'Madama,'* he said, saluting faultlessly, 'I regret to inform you that Sisto Bellini has left Naples. He has just been called by telegram to his home in Brindisi, where his grandmother expects him to close her dying eyes.' 'And what about my bag, Major? My rings?' Then he clicked his heels, raised a hand to his cocked hat, and said with a smile . . . Oh! such a dazzling smile . . . he said . . . What's the matter, Hedwige?"

Her question remained unanswered. Her face livid, Hedwige kept her eyes on a car that had just passed them slowly enough for her to recognize, behind a glass pane, the face that had haunted her for the last four months. A few seconds were sufficient for her to see Gaston Dolange sitting on the cushioned back seat most nonchalantly and by him a gray-headed man who held himself very straight and pointed a gloved finger at the trees in the mall. That was all. The car spun along noiselessly close to the curb, turned right, and crossed the bridge.

As though in a nightmare, Hedwige heard a voice trying to reach her ears, but immense distances separated her from the sound of words. Suddenly, she felt a hand take her arm.

"What's the matter now?" repeated Mme Vasseur. "Would you like to sit down on that bench?"

Hedwige could hear the garrulous voice now, and it forced her back into the cruel, commonplace little world where she struggled, and the first thing that she noticed was the shadows cast over the ground by the bare limbs of the plane trees; it seemed as though she had never seen them as she did then, and, in spite of herself, she admired the strength and delicacy of the black lines crisscrossing at her feet in a skillful tangle that resembled lacework with enlarged and distorted meshes.

Meanwhile, Mme Vasseur led her to a bench where they sat in silence for a short time. Hedwige raised her eyes and took in at a glance a view of the part of town that rose in tiers on a hill across the river: the sun jubilantly gilded the gray houses and lent an air of magnificence to a setting where despair reigned triumphant. She heard Mme Vasseur talking reasonably to her in a kind of tumultuous stillness caused by the sunlight.

"How many times have I told you that you don't eat enough? Only today . . . You're apt to have fits of giddiness. You don't keep up your strength. . . ."

She's seen nothing, thought Hedwige. So much the better.

As soon as they were home again, she went to her room. It had become her battleground. She felt intensely relieved to be in her room again, for there she could grieve, safe from the Vasseurs' foolish twaddle; and what she above all longed for was to carry off, like a living quarry, Gaston Dolange's image to a spot where she could contemplate it at leisure, before time could tarnish it. She had just seen the young man: it had not been thirty minutes since he passed her, and so close that he would have turned his head, if she had called him. And why had she not done so? Because she could not? Such a simple thing was forbidden.

Taking off her hat, she threw herself on the bed and buried her face in the pillow. Ulrique had lied to her, probably for the sake of peace. He had never gone to La Rochelle. He was here, in the same town with her, and breathed the same air. And in the silence, she closed her eyes and saw him once more: he frowned a little and pouted like a child who had been denied a passing fancy; to her mind, this sulky expression improved his looks. Yet, how ugly he seemed, with lips that were too full, too red, and a snub nose! But there was nothing to be done about it, she loved him; she loved his low forehead and obstinate look, everything that might have spoilt his face for another woman perhaps, but had not Ulrique herself said in her cynical voice: ". . . he's far more than handsome, he's irresistibly ugly!"

Time went by, she did not move. Resting her head on her forearms, she feasted on the appearance of a face that moved past her in a second, endlessly, the second when she had seen it on the mall. And whom was M. Dolange with? His father, no doubt.

She rose suddenly and glanced in the mirror on her dressing table. She looked pale, certainly, but tearless. There was more character than charm in the small white face that watched her over a row of bottles, she thought. "Perhaps I'm not very pretty," she murmured. But if she *fixed up* a little, as Ulrique said, if she powdered her face a trifle more skillfully . . . Her face had not been very nicely powdered, the day she talked to Gaston Dolange. The idea devastated her heart. She covered her face with both hands, a familiar gesture, as though to hide, to escape this humiliating memory, but the past remained indestructible, nothing could be done about it. And slowly a thought took shape in her mind: she suffered too much, and suffering was no solution. Then she sat at her dressing table, powdered her face carefully, did her hair, went through all the motions that she judged reasonable, and gradually calmed down.

As Gaston Dolange was still in town, she could at least try to see him. Of course, Ulrique's absence complicated matters, but the name of one of her friends had not fallen into deaf ears, and she remembered Arlette. True, she did not know her, but she had often passed the shop over which this unusual name was inscribed in a showy Victorian script. What prevented her calling on the antique dealer? Ulrique would be furious, but Ulrique was away.

Call on the antique dealer? And why? She brushed the question aside. Arlette knew Gaston Dolange, and that was enough. Under pretense of looking at her furniture, Hedwige would go to see her tomorrow morning; she would know what to say to her, how to make her act, but make her act in what way? That she did not want to know yet, and confined herself to the present, and what she wanted was that something should happen.

She felt better now, and marvelled that she should have managed to scatter such a load of dark clouds by making such an easy decision. Lighting the two small pink lamps on her dressing table, she peered into the mirror with less severity than a few minutes before and gave her reflection a forced smile that she tried to retain and wear like a mask.

A moment later she went down to the dining room, where she found the Vasseurs, Raoul, and Mme Pauque. They were discussing the high cost of living and paid no attention to Hedwige as she took her usual seat at the table. Raoul quoted prices and what he called indices, while Mme Vasseur referred to the cook's account book, then came a massive digression concerning international policies, and Raoul prognosticated. Finally, just as dessert was being finished, Mme Pauque asked whether there had been any news of Jean. A very heavy silence ensued, and Mme Pauque simply raised majestic eyebrows, for the glance that she cast around her furtively met faces that looked like doors, walled up, and forever.

Lost in dreams, Hedwige did not notice what happened around her; for the last half-hour, she had felt happy and stirred with new hopes; and she slept well, that night.

Chapter 3

Next morning, around half-past eleven, she stole out of the old house and crossed the river that separated her from a quarter less venerable than hers, to be sure, but far more amusing and one that zealous tradesmen attempted to make fashionable. A certain free-and-easiness was allowed there, and it had gone so far as to set up a tearoom recently. Ulrique, who had been present at its opening, spoke favorably of that exotic institution. Strictly speaking, tea was not much liked in the town where this story takes place, but its use had become imperative, along with other habits that would have horrified previous generations.

Hedwige knew very little about such things. Scenting from afar the perils of what she called modern times, Mme Vasseur watched over her niece most strictly, although there were sudden gaps due to absent-mindedness; but Ulrique always appeared at the right moment to block the road to danger and completely obstruct its fascinating width. It pleased Ulrique, for somewhat obscure reasons, to lecture a simple soul like Hedwige and to grant her own self every license that did not damage her reputation.

Be it as it may, Ulrique was far away and Hedwige walked gaily to the quay where Arlette's shop was situated. There was a sweetness in the air that made one feel like smiling and the sunlight fondly caressed even the ugliest houses, showing up every tile of a roof as though it were something rare. The fact was that the façades bordering the quay were not without a certain rather heavy dignity that smacked of bourgeois prosperity, a century ago. Arrogant gateways and interminable balconies where whole families could have stood spoke of material success and business briskly transacted till the last gasp. It just happened that Arlette's shop nested under one of these balconies: small, in good taste, painted a Trianon gray, and, over the door, the black lettering previously mentioned, in a sloping Victorian hand.

Hedwige walked by at first without entering and cast an elaborately careless glance at two Directoire armchairs that stood in the shop window looking like a couple of self-satisfied financiers dressed in gray taffeta with a water-green stripe; then, having moved on a few steps, she stopped. What was she going to say to the woman? She could think of nothing, but no doubt the words would come of themselves, as happens in such cases. All of a sudden, she caught sight of herself in a pastry-shop mirror and imagined that she heard Ulrique's affected voice: "You look dressed up, as though you were going to a wedding." Her heart sank: it was true. Far worse: the expression that really described her frock rose to her lips in a moan: "Dressed up in my Sunday best!" Instead of this absurdly dainty, pale blue dress, she should have worn her black frock that hung forsaken in her cupboard at that very moment. All right, I'll go home, she thought despairingly. Instead of which, fired with sudden determination, she walked up to the shop and flung open the door.

Armchairs and chairs disposed around a circular table on which stood a large vase of white flowers gave the place the inviting aspect of a drawing room, and a magnificent Aubusson spread its flowers under the feet of visitors. Hedwige advanced, then stopped short, abashed. From the back of the shop, a lady in black advanced to meet her, elbows close to her sides, hands clasped in a highly reserved attitude. A slim, straight woman, whose age was difficult to guess but whose youth was certainly no more than a memory; above a long, rather sly face, a fringe of golden hair betrayed the fond hope of being attractive, in spite of age, and so did the rouge that touched up thin cheeks and the dark red lipstick that stressed uncompromising lips, those of an old businessman. Half-closed eyes bordered by black lashes, and slit like buttonholes, cast an enigmatical glance at Hedwige, and with a very faint nod that might have passed for a greeting she said:

"Madame . . ."

Hedwige was almost flustered. She had imagined Arlette as a sort of hilarious, obese bacchante.

"I'm Ulrique's cousin," she said awkwardly.

This remark was greeted with a shriek, and in a jingling of bracelets Arlette's hands parted to express surprise and joy before taking Hedwige's. The latter offered no resistance.

"Ulrique's cousin!" repeated Arlette in a voice filled with rich, caressing modulations. "I've wanted to know you for years, and you introduce yourself, just like that, suddenly! Ah! Adorable! Come this way."

Crossing the shop, she led Hedwige to a kind of tent-shaped boudoir where silken divans strewn with cushions gave the illusion, with a little effort, of being in an Eastern bazaar. Hedwige, who had never seen anything of the kind, cast a surprised glance around her which did not escape her watchful hostess.

"I can see that my little nest seems curious to you," said Arlette. "Ulrique adores it because you can see everything that goes on in the shop without being seen by customers. Do sit down—Mademoiselle Hedwige!"

Hedwige sat in a long, low chair that felt unaccountably deep, although she was careful not to remark upon it. She was agitated and could not quite understand what the antique dealer said. Arlette talked with much glibness while she toyed with the big rings that loaded her slim, agile fingers.

"Ulrique and I have been accomplices for such a long time," she said, "for I knew her when she wore her hair in pigtails. How lovely she was with her hair in pigtails! You were too young then to realize it, but you know that she's as interested in you as if you were her sister. She appears to be brusque and distant, at times. That's what I call her sense of modesty, yes, her sense of modesty. Ah! If a customer comes in, I'll put him out! Look, I'm going to treat you as I do Ulrique: I'll remove the shop door handle, so we'll have a little peace. . . ."

She gave a kind of leap and disappeared from the boudoir. Hedwige heard the peremptory sound of the dealer's heels in the shop and took advantage of being alone for a moment to look around her. On a whatnot of Moroccan style, her eye was caught by a row of ten or twelve large volumes in sumptuous parti-colored bindings. She stretched out a timid hand toward the first volume just as Arlette returned unexpectedly.

"You're interested in them, aren't you?" she asked, half lying back on the divan. "Don't you think that

Mardrus' translation of the *Arabian Nights* is wonderful? No? You haven't read it? I'm not sure that it's quite the proper book for a girl, but I'll lend it to you—or you can come here to read it."

Arlette's flow of words dazed Hedwige, who forgot at times why she had come. She recovered her self-possession suddenly when the antique dealer offered her a liqueur.

"No, thank you. It's very kind of you. . . . I have a favor to ask of you. . . ."

Arlette drew herself up very straight, silver decanter in hand, and her lips tightened.

"A favor?" she repeated, scenting a possible danger to her purse.

Hedwige turned very pink.

"Oh!" she said, "it's probably wrong of me to talk to you about this . . . but sometimes one feels so—yes, so lonely."

The words rose to her lips with an effort and seemed extraordinary to her: they were not what she had intended to say to a woman whom she had known for a quarter of an hour. The dealer put the decanter down and grasped both of Hedwige's hands.

"My child!" she murmured effusively, for now that she was reassured, she could freely vent her feelings without running any risks. "I knew there was something the matter."

"Did Ulrique tell you?"

Arlette wrinkled up her blue eyelids.

"Yes," she said. "I know all about it."

There was a short moment of embarrassment. Hedwige hung her head and gently pulled her hands away from the dealer, who gradually released them.

"And now you see that you can confide in me," continued Arlette in her most cordial voice. "It will do you good. What's gone wrong today?"

Two large tears sparkled in Hedwige's eyes.

"Nothing," she whispered, like a child. "Everything. I've lost all hope."

"Come, come," said Arlette, who could no longer control her curiosity, "pretty lips like yours weren't made to say such sad things." She waited a moment and then came out with a sentence that she often used and that could be interpreted as one pleased, according to circumstances: "Everything can always be fixed up."

"You think so?" cried Hedwige, her nose buried in a handkerchief.

"Ha! Ha! Do I think so! It's easy to see you don't know Arlette! But then, you must speak openly to her. Come, Hedwige, tell me all about it, as if I were an old friend."

"I saw him yesterday, he went by in a car, just a yard away from me," said Hedwige at a breath. "He didn't see me," she added in a lower tone.

"Ah? Well, but . . . I don't see what's tragic about that."

"Ulrique told me that he had gone to La Rochelle. It wasn't true. He's here and hasn't made the least attempt to see me. Why should he, anyway?"

"Oh! You know what men are like! Now tell me, do you really find him so attractive?"

"Attractive . . . How strange," murmured Hedwige pensively, "I've never thought of him in that way. I love him, you see." She hung her head as she said this.

"Oh, botheration!" exclaimed Arlette under her breath.

"Didn't you know it?" asked Hedwige, after a short pause.

"The fact is . . . well, no. Ulrique didn't quite keep me informed. She thought there might be a slight flirtation, nothing more." With a sudden gesture that proved more embarrassment than anything else, she seized Hedwige's hands and held them; this time, the girl made no attempt to release them. "My little Hedwige," she pursued, "what's important above all is that you should be happy. Now, it remains to be seen whether this young man is capable of ensuring your happiness. Frankly, I don't think so."

"Now why?"

"Oh, it's a long story. Ulrique herself knew nothing of it and I myself have only just discovered . . ."

"Discovered what?"

It was Hedwige who now spoke with assurance to Arlette. The dealer sat holding her hands like objects that she did not know what to do with, and appeared hopelessly at sea.

"Ah! How can I express it?" Arlette's laugh rang false. "Gaston Dolange comes of a good family . . ." She got up suddenly. "You weren't thinking of marrying him, were you?"

"Why, yes," replied Hedwige, getting up also. "Of course."

"Marriage is another matter."

"I don't understand. . . ."

They looked at each other silently, face to face in the shadowy boudoir, and Arlette finally turned her restless eyes away.

"We might talk all this over later, if you like," she said, raising a hand to her jade necklace and fingering one of the stones. "You might come here . . ."

"No," said Hedwige, "I want to know. You asked me if I was thinking of marriage."

"Of course, one can always get married. . . . Young Dolange will marry sometime or other . . . particularly as he's not well-off and in great need of money. . . ." She paused between each sentence, looking like a hunted animal.

"You mean that he'll marry for money?"

"Yes, that's about it," replied Arlette, suddenly looking jovial. "A money marriage, the shabbiest of solutions, in fact, and one that's quite unworthy of a girl like you, Hedwige, you must marry someone who loves you. . . ." She paused for a second. All the wrinkles with which guile had furrowed her face were gathered into a grimace of tenderness as she rolled her eyes up and looked at the ceiling. "Love is such a pretty thing," she said artlessly.

"No," said Hedwige brusquely, "it's not pretty, it's terrible."

Arlette's lips parted.

"Ah!" she said at last, "you have a passionate nature, you have!" She slipped her hand under Hedwige's arm and drew her gently toward the divan, where they sat down once more.

"I simply adore natures like yours," continued Arlette. "And you see that I'm plain-spoken too, sincere and in love with the Infinite. That's enough to convince you how well I understand you. So I'm going to speak freely to you. You don't smoke? No? There's an obstacle where young Dolange is concerned, Hedwige. The world is full of young men who could make you happy, and you have to come across the very one who can't. Oh! Ulrique, I'm annoyed with you for being so clumsy!"

"Clumsy?"

Arlette stuck a cigarette in a long emerald-green holder.

"Why, rather! She should never have introduced you to that . . ."

"Well," asked Hedwige, in a calm, patient tone, "that what?"

There was a short silence, while Arlette lit a cigarette.

"A young man who can't be attracted by you."

"How do you know?"

Arlette flourished her cigarette holder and her bracelets tinkled on her wrists.

"If you think that such things can be said, just like that! It's not so simple. To begin with, nothing is simple. Particularly nowadays. . . . We're living in such times—since the war. . . . Everything has changed! Morals, especially. Morals!" She waved her hand once more and drew a long puff from her cigarette. "It's incredible, even here, in this town!"

She continued to hold forth for several minutes, punctuating her speech with vigorous exclamations and, the vaguer her words, the more energy she put into their pronunciation.

"You can't imagine," she continued, "you couldn't realize it unless you saw it. And when I think of the things people say . . . You can't be aware of all this, in your house. You live in the past. But it's like a revolution. . . ." She made a slight thrust at a pumpkin-shaped blue cushion.

Hedwige silently stared at the woman who wriggled in her black dress, her movements not unlike those of an animal.

"What are you talking about?" she asked blankly.

Arlette turned her long face toward Hedwige and grew still suddenly, and very attentive.

"You're not such a child as one might think," she

said slowly. "What am I talking about? You might as well ask what I'm trying not to talk about. Come now, I'm sure you've understood me perfectly. You know quite well that young Dolange is not the man for you."

Hedwige got up: "Not for me . . ." she whispered.

"Oh!" said Arlette, reaching out for the decanter, "I should have said: not for us. Will you have a thimbleful of port?"

Hedwige seemed not to have heard. She could scarcely breathe, her head swam, but she made an effort to conceal this from the dealer, for suddenly she despised the woman, just as she despised herself for having confided in a stranger.

"If you looked at him with more detachment, you know," said Arlette, sitting up a little among the cushions, "you'd see that he's just like any other young fellow, no more, no less. . . ."

A cry rose to Hedwige's lips, but she checked it.

"I would like to know," she said, after a hesitation, "what makes you think he's not the man for me—for us . . . as you say."

Arlette poured herself a glass of port. She looked up and peered at Hedwige, who did not stir.

"Ask Ulrique."

"No," said Hedwige. "Tell me. I want to know the truth."

The sound of her own voice filled her with horror: it had a beseechingness about it that heralded tears. Putting her glass down on a brass tray, Arlette rose softly and laid her hand on Hedwige's shoulder.

"It's exactly as if he *could not.* It amounts to that, in any case. Have you understood me, at last?"

"Yes," said Hedwige.

This was not true. For some time, everything the

woman said to her seemed impenetrably obscure. She was frightened: something in her scented danger.

"I must go," she whispered.

"Just as you like." Arlette sighed and took Hedwige by the arm. "But we'll meet again."

"Yes, we'll meet again," repeated Hedwige mechanically.

Leaving the Turkish boudoir, they walked through the shop and stopped at the door.

"Next time," said Arlette with her fist on the door handle, "you must make a luckier choice."

Hedwige started as though she had been struck.

"It's not a question of choosing!" she cried, her eyes shining.

"Perhaps, perhaps. . . . But I know a great many people. . . ." She opened the door and whispered: "Come now, be brave—my darling!"

Hedwige found herself outside, without knowing how. She took a few steps in the wrong direction, turned back, crossed over to avoid passing by the shop, and suddenly hailed a taxi.

Once home and in her bedroom, she removed her hat with the motions of an automaton and sat down at her dressing table. It occurred to her, looking at a face set in a kind of sorrowful amazement, that the girl she saw in the glass was not the one she had seen there the day before. Something extraordinary had taken place. Yet, everything remained as it had been: the ruffles around the dressing table, the bottles and brushes, but she was no longer the same. The girl whom she looked at and who looked at her so attentively had become a stranger. That was perhaps why they stared at each other dumbly, but after a moment they opened their mouths and said aloud:

"It's all over."

The words dropped into a deep silence. Hedwige got up, went to the window, and leant her brow against the pane. There was no one in the courtyard, but the city's hum could be heard in the distance, and this rumor sounded like a threatening voice. Yet, nothing had changed: Hedwige knew the muffled rumble of cars, just as she knew the sunlight on the uneven cobblestones and on the trunk of the linden, but for the past hour everything had taken a new and terrible aspect. I wish I were dead, she thought. Everything around her told her this so clearly that she was surprised not to have thought of it sooner: the thick black line that underscored the whole of the roof, lengthwise, the shape of the windows that faced hers, the shadow that filled the high, vaulted passage leading to the carriage entrance, and even the tender blue of a sky over which tattered clouds scurried, everything took on the same meaning, articulated the same words, those that she could not drive out of her head: I wish I were dead. Her eyes were dry and her jaws tightened a little; she felt cold, but stood perfectly still, as though she feared that a single false step might make her fall into a precipice. Almost a quarter of an hour went by, then someone knocked at her door.

That afternoon, Mme Pauque was more attentive than usual to Hedwige and far more affable. She guessed, perhaps, that something had gone wrong.

"My little girl," she said, "you're very pale. I'm sure you need some fresh air. We'll go out together."

"No," said Hedwige.

"Come," said Mme Pauque, taking her gently by the elbow, "I see very well that you're worried. A walk will divert you, even if you don't feel like talking. A change of ideas is so important when one is in trouble. You are grieving, aren't you?" she asked in a most solicitous voice, her lovely ink-black eyes staring into Hedwige's. The latter turned her head away.

"Leave me alone," whispered Hedwige.

Mme Pauque slipped a firm arm around her niece's waist.

"I could never forgive myself that," she said, leading Hedwige to the door.

They went out. Contrary to her determination, Hedwige offered no resistance. Lightly clad, for it was a warm afternoon, they walked toward the river and Mme Pauque was tactful enough not to break Hedwige's silence until they had passed the entrance gates of an almost deserted public park. Clumps of laurel and privet bordered long, meandering, placid walks, and the trees wore a kind of mantilla of tiny leaves through which the light beamed tenderly. This peaceful, rather dull setting seemed admirably adapted to confidences.

"My little Hedwige," began Mme Pauque, "we've all gone through the same experiences. I've been young myself and I know what is troubling you. An unfortunate love affair."

"I'd rather not talk about it," said Hedwige, a little hoarsely.

"What more natural?" asked Mme Pauque in her blandest accents.

They sat on a bench and Hedwige bent her head, endeavoring to hide the tears that wet her cheeks. It was then that Mme Pauque discreetly opened her bag and took out a handkerchief which she silently offered her niece. There was a silence, an odor of heliotrope floated in the air, and Hedwige blew her nose. At that moment,

Mme Pauque opened her bag once more and produced a letter, holding it in such a manner as to conceal the address.

"My child," she said, "we're going to be reasonable. This letter was delivered this morning, while you were out. It comes from Naples and is addressed to you. Needless to tell you, I don't know its contents, but without being a witch I can guess that it's from Jean. Now, we have learned some very unpleasant things about him, and it is better for you not to know about them."

"Unpleasant things?" asked Hedwige, raising a shiny little nose.

"Oh! You'll know later on. . . . Life is full of mean, ugly deeds, as you'll find out for yourself quite soon enough. Will you allow me to open this letter and read it to you? I can see that my request surprises you."

For Hedwige had already stretched out a hand to take the letter and remained open-mouthed with astonishment, but on second thought, what could it matter if Mme Pauque read her letter from Jean? There was only one person in the whole world that counted for her.

"I don't mind," she said, letting her hand drop.

"Very well," replied Mme Pauque, immediately tearing open the envelope and unfolding three large sheets of paper covered with an even writing.

"My dear little Hedwige," she began, *"I am writing to you this evening because I feel lonely, sad, and uneasy in this foreign town where, after a few dazzling hours, nothing can appeal to me here again. I miss you. It may seem strange to you, perhaps, that I should be talking to you like this, I who find it so hard to confide in anyone, but you must remember the time when I came to see you in your room."*

Mme Pauque looked up from the letter and turned to Hedwige.

"Yes," said the latter, "he came to see me a few months before he went away. Why, I've never been able to understand. He simply told me that he had been in great trouble."

"Great trouble? What kind of trouble?"

"That's what he wouldn't tell me."

"Humph!" exclaimed Mme Pauque. "We'll let it go at that."

She continued: *"At that time, I needed to talk to someone pure, as you are. Oh! Don't protest! You can't possibly fathom the power of innocence over a man like myself . . ."*

Mme Pauque skimmed over the next lines with a distrustful eye before reading them aloud.

". . . over a man like myself who feels general hostility increasing around him."

"What does he mean?" asked Hedwige, with sudden interest. "He's always so mysterious."

"Very," said Mme Pauque.

"At any rate, it was better for me to leave a town that I love for reasons which I cannot tell you, but where danger prowls around me day and night. My words probably seem very obscure to you, and I want them to be so, for I would not venture to write you if I thought you could guess my meaning. I would be sick with shame, and yet I want to talk to you, and to you only. . . ."

Hedwige could not refrain from a gesture, as though she wanted to snatch a letter that was quite obviously addressed to her alone, but Mme Pauque moved away slightly and continued very quickly:

"I should probably go to confession, if I had greater faith. There is no lack of churches. But, alas, facilities reserved for pious souls are not for me. I'm suffering, Hedwige. I'm suffering because I'm in love, as you are. We have this bond between us, a bond so strong that I cannot break it. If I told you the name of the person I love, you could not bear it and you would swell the ranks of my enemies, who will never forgive me for being the way that God created me."

"Can you understand a word of all this?" asked Hedwige.

Mme Pauque cast a sharp glance at her over the letter, which she held with both hands, and crossed her feet.

"Let's go on with this," she said.

"To love without being loved is more than I can bear. . . ."

Hedwige burst out sobbing.

"Poor Jean!" she cried, her face in her handkerchief.

"Pull yourself together," said Mme Pauque. "Some people are coming this way."

"I'd rather you gave me the letter."

"Certainly, I'll give it to you once we've read it. It's my duty to acquaint myself with its contents, for someone must watch over you, Hedwige."

"I'm not a child."

"You're not a child, but Jean is a wicked man," said Mme Pauque evenly.

"A wicked man!"

"Would you like me to go on with the letter? I'll wait first until these people have passed by."

An old lady leaning on a schoolboy's arm walked slowly by. "You must write to her this evening," said the old lady. "It's been such a time since she . . ." But the boy was looking at Hedwige and did not answer.

A moment after, Mme Pauque cast a glance over her shoulder and went on with a kind of energy that reminded one of a horseman charging down a long avenue:

"In my struggle against despair, I had recourse to what is termed pleasure, the most sinister thing in the world when your heart is not in it and your youth is far behind you. I lived dangerously, as people say. I hoped for a misfortune and dreaded it at the same time. It happened. Fate obliged me to leave our town and I sought refuge in this one where not a glance from anyone gives me a little of the happiness we all look for. I live in poverty, but would accept this trial gladly (listen, Hedwige), if I could only get back my former suffering and once again see a face whose memory is a torture that I will not even attempt to describe.

"Having talked about myself thus, it may appear strange and quite out of place to you, if I write the name of Gaston Dolange. . . ."

A cry escaped Hedwige's lips. Mme Pauque looked gravely at her and continued:

"You know him too slightly and your idea of him is too far removed from the truth for me to convince you by what I am about to say, but I beseech you not to attempt to see him again. Try, on the contrary, to forget him, for he can only be the cause of your shedding the bitterest and the most useless tears that ever reddened a woman's eyes."

"My poor child," said Mme Pauque kindly.

Hedwige was silent for a moment, then asked in a low voice:

"Is there anything else?"

"No," said Mme Pauque, folding the letter and slipping it into the envelope, "he just sends you his love."

She rose, and Hedwige mechanically did the same. They walked quietly toward the park gates, and Mme Pauque attracted Hedwige's attention to a forsythia, where a promise of flowers was announced by golden stitches that formed a kind of constellation. There was a long silence until they reached the avenue that they had left a moment before, then Mme Pauque cleared her throat and said with studied sweetness:

"Don't you think that we should tear this letter up and that I should throw it into a sewer? That's the proper place for it, in my opinion."

"Yes," said Hedwige.

The letter was taken out of Mme Pauque's bag.

"I'll keep the stamp for one of my charities," said Mme Pauque, removing the little colored square from the envelope. After which, she tore the letter into four, then eight pieces, with quiet, precise movements, and threw them, as she had proposed, into a sewer. A bit of paper hesitated on the edge of the great dark opening, and she pushed it in with the tip of her shoe, took Hedwige's arm, and began to talk in a sensible, measured tone that seemed to put things in their proper place.

"It was best to settle matters once and for all," she said. "We've turned over a new leaf, my little Hedwige. Now we can face the future with greater serenity. See how things turn out. This letter whose contents were unknown to me has opened my eyes, not to the wretched Jean—I have no desire to cast stones at him—but to the man you are interested in."

She stopped suddenly and, with a shade of anxiety in her dark eyes, looked attentively at Hedwige:

"For I suppose you have understood?"

"Yes," replied Hedwige.

What she had at last understood was, in Arlette's words, that Gaston Dolange *could not.* Her whole conversation with the antique dealer and the letter which had just been thrown into the sewer had led her to that conclusion, and she knew the name given to this infirmity but did not even even dare mention it to herself. As she walked at Mme Pauque's side, she prevented herself from thinking, much as though she had held her breath, for to think about such things made her feel like screaming.

"I'm glad to see that you are brave and reasonable," said Mme Pauque. "Life is so unkind, Hedwige. However, there will be a compensation, I'm certain of that. You must be strong-minded enough not to think about that little wretch any more."

Why does she insult him? wondered Hedwige. After thinking this over for a few seconds, she asked aloud: "Why do you insult him?"

"What respect could I have for a man who is unworthy of the name?"

Hedwige turned crimson. How could anyone bear Gaston Dolange a grudge for an inborn misfortune? She wanted to answer, but the fear of being led to use embarrassingly precise terms made her hold her tongue. The walk ended silently.

Chapter 4

HEDWIGE DID NOT JOIN the Vasseurs that evening. A meal that she scarcely touched was brought up to her room, but she left the door ajar, in order to feel less lonely, and this allowed her to hear a hum of voices rising from the ground floor. The sound, in turn serious and playful, comforted her a little and drove away an undefinable presence.

Downstairs was a guest that Hedwige did not know, a man of some importance in the political world. She had no idea why he was dining with the Vasseurs, nor was she much interested. So she had eagerly agreed not to be present, as prominent people always made her a little shy, but listened with a kind of gratitude to Mme Vasseur's artificial laugh as it greeted the guest of honor's witticisms. For the last hours, she had been in such agitation that the outside world seemed to make her feel safe. She dreaded that someone might talk to her, that she might be torn away from herself, and yet she needed a little human excitement around her for, in some unaccountable manner, it cheered her. The idea that the household would, sooner or later, settle down to sleep threw her into a kind of panic. She would have liked to hear the sound of people talking all through the night.

Dressed in a long white woollen dressing gown, she ventured as far as the landing and sat on the top step of the staircase leading down to the hall. The darkness around her was not so thick that she could not distinguish a great oval window through which branches of trees could be seen vaguely, but the sky was black. Gradually, she recognized the pattern of the oak banisters that stood out against the white wall. This was the oldest part of the house and retained an appearance of austere prosperity characteristic of certain provincial dwellings. Generations of men and women had walked up these stairs, and she could not help thinking of all the hope and all the dread that had circulated in this space and at a period long since forgotten. Who could say if a woman had not sat on this step, as she did, a prey to the same anxiety? And without daring to admit why, she glanced around her.

Snatches of loud conversation made her start. Something was being discussed and bits of sentences could be heard above a great din, which was like the baying of hounds: "No one can say . . ." "For over fifty years . . . Not so fast . . . It's the first time that such an affair . . ."

Hedwige did not attempt to understand, but her heart thumped, as though the words concerned her. The uproar soon died down and the conversation fell back into a vague reassuring buzz. She leant her brow against one of the thick banisters that supported the handrail and, closing her eyes, suddenly saw Gaston Dolange's face once more. He was not looking at her. Had he ever looked at her? Had he ever seen her, even the day when Ulrique had introduced him to her? Probably, she no more existed in his eyes than a tree or a chair, whereas she feasted on the terrible contempt that she read on his sulky lips and in light eyes where boredom seemed to lurk. She examined his features as one wanders in memory through a landscape where one has suffered. Who was he? Whom did he love? Something roused her suddenly, a frantic desire to throw her arms around him, and she leapt to her feet panting, both hands at her throat. At that moment, she heard a cry that seemed unending, a great cry of anguish and fear that beat against the walls and, almost as astounded as horrified, she recognized her own voice. This scandalous, terrible appeal rose from her own throat.

She stopped and the blood rushed to her face. Not a sound came up from the dining room, where people no doubt wondered what this meant, then Mme Vasseur's society voice was heard. Raoul expressed an opinion which was immediately taken up by the others, and after a short hesitation conversation started up again.

Now she was once more in her room, groping her way among the furniture. She did not want to turn on the light, what she wanted was to hide in the dark, to creep between her sheets and remain motionless, as though she were dead. And this way, night would bring her to day, and when it grew light, everything would be changed: she would suffer in a different manner.

She kept the same position for over fifteen minutes, her cheek in a pillow that turned boiling hot, and a word that she had withheld for a long time rose to her lips, a word that she would never have dared utter before anyone and that she whispered so low that she could scarcely hear the sound of the shameful syllables:

"Impotent . . ."

She had a dream. He stood naked before her. His body gleamed like that of an idol, and she saw his breast and hips throb as though he had been running, but he did not move: he waited. A singular expression swept over his features, first through his blue eyes, in which she thought to read a challenge, then over the full lips lightly stretched in a ferocious grin that showed teeth white as a child's. Some time went by. Hedwige felt an intolerable burning throughout her flesh and nothing in her was alive except for eyes that followed the young man's glance, and sometimes this glance went right, sometimes left, but never in her direction, and she screamed with all her might, screamed with horror, screamed without cease. Then came a shadow that concealed the apparition and she gradually recognized Jean's face. He opened his mouth, but never a sound came out of it, no matter what pains he took to articulate clearly, and over his tear-furrowed cheeks she saw two thin trickles of blood that flowed from his eyes. He sadly shook his head, arms stretched out to keep her back, not to welcome her. She called him. Jean looked down at the floor, and there were the fragments of the letter that Mme Pauque had torn up, and he vanished. After him, Arlette stood between the motionless young man and herself, saying: "No!" in a rough, unkind voice. Finally, came Mme Pauque, dressed in black from head to foot, majestic and beautiful, arms raised like a prophetess: "You are blind!" she cried. "Hedwige is blind!" "Oh!" moaned Hedwige. "It's not true! No! No!"

"Yes!" continued Mme Pauque gently, stroking her hair. "You must wake up, child. You're having a nightmare, but all is well, it's over. Wake up!"

She patted Hedwige's shoulder as she said this, until the girl escaped from a dream that had not made her cry out in terror, as she thought, but moan plaintively like a sick child. A shiver went over her. She turned over on her back, opened her eyes wide, and stared at the face that she had left in a nightmare to meet again in waking life.

"Come," said Mme Pauque, pushing back locks of hair from her niece's brow, "calm yourself, my little girl. You're in your room and I'm here by you."

"I dreamt about you," said Hedwige.

"Was I so dreadful?" asked Mme Pauque, laughing. "What could I have been doing in your dream?"

But Hedwige could no longer remember anything. With increasing irritation, she tried to retain the last vestiges of a nightmare that faded from her mind, leaving a wound behind it.

"You're a little feverish," said Mme Pauque. "I'll give you some aspirin. That will make you sleep."

She disappeared. The little lamp at Hedwige's bedside shed an amber-colored light that softly touched the flowered wallpaper and buff linen curtains, whose long straight folds looked like stone columns. This was the familiar setting that Hedwige loved and hated at the same time and mentally called her battleground, but that evening she felt as though she had found it again after a long absence, a hard, dark journey through unknown regions. She vaguely thought over these things for a minute or two. The ticking of a small alarm clock at her side filled the silence. She listened to the sound for a moment, then got up and ran a comb through her hair. I must do all this, she thought, because living means going through all these gestures. . . .

Mme Pauque returned at that instant, holding a bottle of aspirin.

"I have no fever," said Hedwige.

Mme Pauque looked at her attentively: "Oh yes, you

have," she said, "your eyes are shiny. But I won't try to influence you." She waited a few seconds and added: "I'm afraid you won't sleep tonight."

"That's of no importance," replied Hedwige brusquely, "nothing has any importance."

"What are you going to do?" whispered Mme Pauque. "It's past midnight."

"I shall lie down. Probably I'll read a little."

She sank onto the bed; an expression that verged on fury beautified her: lips parted, eyes enlarged by purple shadows, she stared fixedly at her visitor. Mme Pauque brought a chair close to Hedwige and sat down.

"My reason for coming to see you," she said gently, "is that I heard the scream, while we were at dinner. Raoul wanted to send someone up here. I prevented him. I knew only too well what the matter was. You needed to be alone. Did I do the right thing?"

Hedwige nodded. Mme Pauque leant forward and took her hand with extreme delicacy.

"My little girl," she said, "I too have suffered. I know. Life is cruel, but time heals wounds. Try not to think about that wretched young man any longer. He's not worthy of you."

"Not worthy of me!" cried Hedwige, on the verge of tears. "What does that mean? I didn't ask that he should be worthy of me, I wanted him to love me."

"But he can't love you. Imagine what a disaster such a marriage would have been, what people would have thought, the disgrace . . . It must not be said that we associate with such people. . . ."

"Such people! It's not his fault."

"Don't try to find excuses for him, my child. No, please," she added, as Hedwige made a gesture. "I refuse to talk about such shameful things."

Hedwige withdrew her hand and remained silent.

"You should be told that, where Jean is concerned, this sad specimen of humanity will never live here again. I think it better so. An important person has been good enough to assume the responsibility of hushing up a very ugly business, and the newspapers, thank Heaven, won't mention it."

She bent her head for an instant and continued:

"As you've already guessed, this is the man who dined with us tonight. He has promised to use his influence at the *préfecture*. You can't have too many friends, as you see. At all events, we're rid of that wicked man."

"What wicked man?" asked Hedwige.

"My child, I wonder whether you're in a fit state to understand what I'm saying. I'm talking of Jean."

"But what has he done?"

Mme Pauque got up, rather impatiently.

"You can question Ulrique when she returns," she muttered.

She brushed Hedwige's burning forehead with dry lips and stood up very straight. How beautiful she looked, the lamp on the bedside table lighting up her motionless face from beneath! Her perfect features were serene as a goddess', her magnificently bright eyes shone like jet.

"I loathe scandal," she said, looking at the wall, as though she were addressing some invisible person, "and there shall be no scandal in this house." She looked down at Hedwige and said: "Go to sleep, my child."

And leaving the room at once, she closed the door with care, as though to avoid breaking the silence of night.

Next morning, Hedwige looked in the glass at a face ravaged by suffering and, for the first time, had a foreboding of what she would be like when life had done its work. For a few seconds, she had a vision of an old woman and turned from the dressing table, horror-stricken. Those swollen eyelids, straight, hard lips, and, more than anything else, the dull, lusterless expression that lurked in hollow eye sockets—could this wasted face be hers? She hesitated, irresolute, took a few steps toward the window, then ran to the bathroom and opened one of the washstand faucets wide. She felt then as though ice burned her cheeks, brow, and mouth, but the pain made amends for what she had seen and she wanted to hide that prophetic mask in consuming flames.

As she wiped her face, a sudden fit of giddiness forced her to sit down on the edge of the bath. If I could die, she thought, die right here, now . . .

She washed, did her hair, and dressed, avoiding a glance at the dressing table. What was important was to come and go as usual, even with that strange pain in her breast which had not left her for several days now. But what was she to do, now she had dressed? She had nothing to do but suffer. The thought struck her like a revelation as she laid her hand on the doorknob. As a rule, she went to see Ulrique, who snubbed her; then she went out with Mme Vasseur or Mme Pauque, or she read a novel in a corner of the morning room. She suddenly realized the emptiness of her life. She was waiting for a husband. She ate and drank, slept, washed, and none of it had any meaning but to keep her well and healthy until her wedding day, happy or not. And now, this important event had taken place: her eyes had been opened, she wanted to die because she was in love with an impotent man. So, from then on, everything took on another meaning.

Someone went by her door. She flung it open and saw the dressmaker, who started and murmured:

"Good morning, Mademoiselle."

What an ugly, dreary sight she was, and how guilty she looked in her shiny, wrinkled little black suit, with a shapeless pancake on her gray head that masqueraded as a hat! Félicie, whom no one ever thought of without being reminded of Mme Vasseur's apt comparison: a small animal, a mouse, yes, that was it, a mouse that was terrified to death!

"Good morning," said Hedwige gloomily.

The dressmaker threw her a frightened glance and went upstairs, her skirt rustling, her arm on the banisters. Two or three seconds after, she had disappeared. A singular idea crossed the girl's mind: She would go up to see Félicie. Why? To know when her jacket would be finished? A deeper reason determined her to follow the dressmaker, but she would not admit it, even to herself: it pleased her, that morning, to make the ill-favored little creature feel slightly uneasy. With a kind of eagerness that resembled joy, she bounded up the stairs and opened the door on the top floor just as Félicie had closed it.

"My jacket," she said.

The dressmaker had raised her arms to take off her hat. She turned to Hedwige, open-mouthed.

"It seems to me that you work more slowly than you did," said Hedwige haughtily, with intonations copied from Ulrique. "You have been at that jacket for weeks."

"It's on account of the braiding, Mademoiselle," replied Félicie, moving away a little toward the end of the room.

Anxiety made her flick her little black eyes this way and that, and she ran the tip of her tongue over her lower lip. She removed her hat and jacket in the twinkling of an eye and, drawing a black apron from her bag, tied it around her waist.

"I'm working," she said.

"You're working," answered Hedwige, her nostrils spreading like an animal sniffing blood. "Just show me your work."

Félicie trotted to the bed where the garment in question lay, with outstretched arms, and then fitted it on Blanchonnet, which stood triumphantly on a corner of the table, with its chest thrown out.

"Mademoiselle can see for herself," said Félicie.

She put on her pince-nez and stroked Blanchonnet's hip with her rough little hand. Hedwige seemed displeased and kept a dreadful silence. Something that she could not quite account for prompted her to humiliate the woman who stood before her, like a culprit before a judge. With a mere word, Hedwige could make this insignificant little person tremble. She thought for a moment and allowed the following sentence to drop from her lips:

"I hope you have a lot of good customers besides us, Félicie."

"Oh!" cried the dressmaker, sticking her fingers into the folds of her apron. "Mademoiselle does not mean to say . . ."

"Yes, I do," said Hedwige, with a weary sigh. "Perhaps . . ."

Félicie did not answer. A little quiver shook her gray head right, then left, and she opened her mouth but not a sound came out of it, a tear sparkled behind her pince-nez, a small tear of anger and despair that hesitated on the tips of her eyelashes before rolling down her flat, pink cheek.

"It's quite possible that someday you might be asked to leave," said Hedwige majestically.

"Asked to leave . . ."

The term, threatening and polite at the same time, hit Félicie like a slap.

"Come now, be brave," said Hedwige. "You'll find work elsewhere."

She looked at the dressmaker's grieved face and thought: She's frightened and she's suffering, she's suffering a lot. And she's wondering what's going to become of her, just like me.

To her great astonishment, Félicie suddenly darted a sly, sharp look at her.

"It's not true," she whispered, "it's not true that Madame wants to dismiss me. I would have known about it. We know everything that goes on, belowstairs. We know everything, Mademoiselle Hedwige."

At that moment, Hedwige felt her heart thump, as though an extremely important event were about to happen. A sudden flush spread over her face and she hung her head.

"Why did you say that, Mademoiselle Hedwige?"

The question was not asked unkindly, but in a humble, timid voice that brought a lump to Hedwige's throat. Tears started from her eyes.

"Now, now," said Félicie, touching her arm, "if you think we don't know everything!"

"Don't know what?" asked Hedwige, blowing her nose.

"Well . . . everything, Mademoiselle."

There was a silence during which the two women looked at each other without realizing that they stood, panting a little, by the dummy as it towered over them in its pretentious, fussy jacket.

"I don't grasp what you mean," stammered Hedwige. "I don't understand."

"Oh!" replied Félicie, "when a lovely girl like you looks so unhappy, it's easy enough to guess what it's all about. And then, you know well enough that servants are neither deaf nor blind. Herbert couldn't believe his eyes when he saw Monsieur . . ."

"Monsieur who?"

The dressmaker removed her pince-nez and thrust out her head slightly.

"Well . . . Monsieur Dolange."

Hedwige instinctively drew back.

"I won't have you mention Monsieur Dolange," she said in a muffled voice, but she lied, she longed with her whole heart to have him mentioned, and she knew that something was about to be said that she dreaded to hear.

"It's hard luck that you should have run across a young man like him," continued Félicie. "Another, any other, but not that one, not Monsieur Jean's friend."

"Monsieur Jean?"

"Yes. Upstairs, they didn't know. They never know anything. But us, belowstairs, we suspected it. Herbert knew, because he's on good terms with the baker's wife. And then, there was that scene in the courtyard. Didn't you hear about it? You were out, perhaps, and of course no one told you of it."

"No. I don't understand, I know nothing. . . ."

"Naturally, a girl shouldn't know about such things," said Félicie, putting her arm around Blanchonnet's waist.

A fiendish smile slowly wrinkled her small face, and Hedwige could scarcely recognize it.

"A well-brought-up young girl doesn't know about

such things," continued the dressmaker, "but we do, belowstairs."

"Please tell me."

"So it's true that you don't know why Monsieur Jean left town suddenly?" whispered the dressmaker.

"Why, no."

"And you don't know either what kind of person Monsieur Dolange is?"

Hedwige looked like an animal that feels a trap closing in on it.

"Why are you talking to me about Monsieur Dolange?"

"Because Monsieur Dolange was Monsieur Jean's friend."

Hedwige grew white. She leaned against the table.

"Well?" she breathed.

"Don't you understand?" asked the dressmaker with a conniving laugh.

"No."

Once more, there was a long silence between them. Hedwige could hear the blood buzzing in her ears.

"I would like you to tell me," she said finally in a toneless voice. "No one ever tells me anything. I didn't know that Monsieur Jean knew Monsieur Dolange . . . but I can't see what's so extraordinary about that."

Félicie took a step toward her and assumed a confidential tone: "If I were you, I'd look around me, Mademoiselle Hedwige. There's no lack of gentlemen in this town. But it's no good thinking of men like Monsieur Jean or Monsieur Dolange."

"What's the matter with Monsieur Jean?" asked Hedwige, drawing back a little.

"Monsieur Jean is like Monsieur Dolange!" cried Félicie, with sudden irritation. And without stopping to think and out of all patience, she declared: "If you don't understand, I won't be the one to tell you, Mademoiselle! To begin with, such things can't be said."

She put on her pince-nez and stared boldly at Hedwige, who blushed.

Hedwige was on the point of asking a question, but checked herself: there was something defiant in the dressmaker's attitude and in the very obscureness of her speech that seemed like a threat, and a terrifying one. She smiled mechanically, and the smile clung to her face, like a mask. She made an awkward gesture, stretched her hand toward the dummy as though to touch the sleeve of her jacket, and after a hesitation, left the room.

Once she was back in her bedroom, she stood motionless at the window, thinking. Her heart still thumped, but she made an effort to grow calm, clasping her hands tightly behind her back, as she did when she was a child and wanted to hold her own against her parents or a teacher who scolded her. In the courtyard, the concierge was sweeping with a big straw broom that made a sound like a waterfall. She listened for a moment, then sat down at a little table and, taking a sheet of monogrammed blue paper from a chintz box, wrote the following letter:

"My dear Jean, I would be most unfeeling if I did not answer a letter like yours, for I realize that you are suffering and, unfortunately, know only too well what that means, at this very moment, when I am writing to you. You are the only one to talk to me as though I were grown up, for, where the rest of the world is concerned, it goes without saying that I am a child; so I find your letter less obscure than you seem to imagine,

and even if I still lack the experience my elders are so proud of possessing, I have recently discovered a great deal about the human heart and the vanity of the hopes I might entertain.

"You are unhappy: I am more unhappy still: I don't know whom you love, but that person may very well be touched someday by your feelings, and it's not impossible for you to continue to believe in happiness. That, as far as I am concerned, is impossible. For I am in love with a man who cannot love me."

At that moment, she let her head drop on her arms and began to sob. For a few minutes, this sound filled the silence of the little room. Her shoulders shaking, Hedwige cried with a kind of violent haste, and little childlike screams escaped her. She panted, suffocating as though she had been plunged into cold water, and, stopping suddenly, blew her nose, picked up the pen which had fallen on the carpet, and continued her letter:

"You know who I mean, and in my present state, I think it would be too much for me to write his name on this paper, but, as it seems that you are his friend, you can measure all the cruelty of a fate that led him to me, so that I could see him and lose my heart to his face, his eyes, and, yes, it is ridiculous to say, fall in love with his hair, his mouth, his hands. Oh! Jean, I am in such pain. I would like to die. I will have to die because his mouth will never be able to tell me that it loves me. Life is too hard. I do not see how anyone could manage to get from hour to hour with this weight. I am not angry with this man, as nature has created him in such a fashion that . . ." She crossed out the last sentence and replaced it by this one: *"I am*

not angry with this man because he cannot return the love of any woman, but I am angry with the pitiless fate that is crushing me."

She put her pen down, paused, and then added:

"And now, I am ashamed of what I am about to write and you are going to find me lacking in pride, but I have suffered too much to know what pride means. I want to see the man I am in love with, I want to see him again. Listen, Jean. I am not as ignorant of the facts of life as you suppose, but I cannot believe what has been hinted to me. Something in me refuses to believe it. In any case, although I cannot change his nature, I can at least try to touch his heart by talking to him. He will love me, Jean, his heart will love me. I beg you to write to him. That is what I dared not ask you a moment ago. Tell him that I will meet him wherever he likes, in the public park at dusk, for instance, tell him no matter what, but contrive to have me see him again."

She lost her head a little as she wrote the last lines and stopped suddenly, wondering whether it would not be better to tear up the whole letter and write it all over again, but her strength failed her. In an almost illegible hand, she scrawled: *"Much love,"* signed her name, and, without pausing for a minute, hurried to a post office, dreading that she might change her mind, as she sometimes did, and think better of it at the last moment. Later on, she would have plenty of time to wonder whether she had acted wisely or foolishly, but she must act first, and think things over afterwards. For she knew only too well that to think things over meant keeping the letter and remaining silent, when she wanted to call for help. So having stuck stamps on the envelope, she threw it into a letter box and went home.

Once more in her room, she drew the window curtains, calmly removed her hat, and sat down at the dressing table: "I've acted," she said aloud to her reflection that silently moved its lips. Her bosom heaved slightly, and in the silence of the little room she repeated the word "acted" with more vigor and precision. It comforted her to hear her own voice. She noticed that her cheeks were pink, her eyes bright. Where was the old woman whom she thought she had seen that morning, in this same mirror? A girl with pleasant features smiled at her, even though the girl needed powder on her forehead and nose, needed to "fix herself up," as Ulrique said. She began to laugh to herself as she lightly ran the puff over her face. What a strange idea to be looking at herself in the failing light! However, she saw well enough and the dusk made her look prettier, lent depth to her eyes. He wouldn't think me so bad-looking, she thought, in this light. What a good thing I said: at dusk. I'm prettier then. . . . How long would it take the letter to reach Naples and for Jean to write to Gaston Dolange? What would the latter do when he received Jean's letter? She paused suddenly, the powder puff poised on her forehead. What would he do? Why, he would write, of course, she would have a letter within ten days, within a week. Till then, she would have to go on living, or pretend to go on living: talk to the Vasseurs, to Mme Pauque, come and go, take walks, wait. She gave a moan. To wait was beyond her strength, to wait was not living, it was dying.

That afternoon, she returned to the post office to find out when her letter would reach Naples. Forty-eight hours. . . . Five had already elapsed, no doubt, but time did not go by fast enough, time ground down the soul of those who waited, as she did. She pictured her letter travelling from hand to hand, in stations, in Italian post offices, finally reaching the hotel where someone would give it to Jean, and then . . . How surprised he would be to know that she suffered in this manner. No, he would not be surprised. He knew. Perhaps she should have dwelt more lengthily on the subject. She would write again. But Jean would understand: was he not suffering in the same way? "Not as much as I am," she murmured. And she tried to imagine Jean's grief, since he was in grief; but she could not. In her mind, she saw a black-eyed woman, very elegant and very cruel, shrieking with laughter at the poor man's declaration of love, and Jean leaving France on that account. Very likely he had not expressed himself as he should, and also, he was not very attractive, what with his awkwardness and serious appearance, whereas the other, Gaston Dolange . . . She stopped short: she had not thought of Gaston Dolange for over five minutes, and blushed, as though she had been unfaithful.

Dinner, that evening, began by being a far more silent meal than usual, but Hedwige was scarcely aware of it, lost as she was in a dream that continually led her away from the dining room, where the wallpaper was imitation Cordova leather and the furniture did its best to recall the most sumptuous period of the French Renaissance. It was sultry weather, and through the open windows the city's muffled roar sounded like a great, indistinct voice continually repeating the same thing. Mme Vasseur and Mme Pauque occasionally exchanged a few words in a confidential tone, but neither Raoul nor M. Vasseur opened his lips except to eat. A short time before the last course, however, and just as the manservant had left the room, Raoul pushed away his plate testily and said aloud:

"To my mind, Ulrique is inexcusable."

"Ulrique was never aware of anything," said Mme Vasseur.

"Her place is here," said Raoul. "She went away because she was frightened."

"I beg of you—" said M. Vasseur, with a nod at Hedwige.

"Oh! She'll have to know about it," continued Raoul. "This is not the kind of thing that can be kept secret."

Mme Vasseur rose, as he said this: "I shall leave the room, if you don't stop."

"Very well," replied Raoul. "I won't say another word."

The manservant returned with a dish of pears stewed in wine. Hedwige looked up at Mme Vasseur as the latter sat down again.

"What's the matter?" she asked. "Has anything happened?"

"Don't bother your head about that, my little girl," said M. Vasseur gently. "I'm quite sure that everything will be all right."

His expression was so sad as he turned to her that it lent his face a kind of majesty. The meal ended without any further conversation, then they went, as usual, to the drawing room, but after a few minutes Mme Vasseur left, followed by Raoul, who wanted to talk to her about having the roof done over, he said.

When she was alone with M. Vasseur and Mme Pauque, Hedwige could not help from glancing around her, as though she expected someone to come in. The room was lofty and magnificently proportioned and seemed all the larger that evening because of the lighting: a single lamp on a round, marble-topped table put a patch of gold in the dusk, but the presence of sofas and armchairs grouped in corners could be vaguely distinguished and the pale blue satin curtains gleamed faintly under the festooned cornices. It was in this room that Mme Vasseur's receptions took place, and it was here, by a rococo console topped by a Venetian looking glass, that Hedwige had talked to Gaston Dolange. She instinctively turned her eyes toward that splendid mirror, with the unreasonable hope that it still held the reflection of a beloved face, but that part of the room was too shadowy, it was too dark around her and those she sat with, and whose hands she examined with a mixture of anger and sadness, because she resented everybody for not being the man she was in love with. In a sort of unintelligible murmur, she heard M. Vasseur express himself in short sentences, interrupted by brief pauses. Mme Pauque said nothing; an amethyst sparkled on her lovely white hands as she rubbed them together.

Finally, M. Vasseur rose and swiftly kissed Hedwige's brow; she started, as though she had been suddenly awakened.

"Good night, my child," he said. "My sister-in-law will explain it all to you much better than I could, but I'm very fond of you, as you know."

He pressed her arm awkwardly and left the room. Mme Pauque rose at that moment. Without haste, she went to one of the windows and half opened it, after drawing the curtains. The innocent odor of lime blossoms stole into the room.

"My child," said Mme Pauque affectionately, "we are obliged to grow accustomed to certain ideas that surprise us at first, and I think that you will be greatly astonished to hear what I am about to tell you."

Hedwige did not understand a word of this sentence. She looked at Mme Pauque's elegant silhouette as it moved to and fro in the faint light and wondered if she were not dreaming.

"As you know," said Mme Pauque as she walked toward the round table with the lamp and sat down again, "nothing in life is ever quite permanent. Everything moves. It is a kind of law. Yesterday, we were talking about Jean, weren't we? Jean had a room in this house, on the top floor."

"Well?" asked Hedwige. "He's in Naples, isn't he?"

Mme Pauque's long, delicate hand moved a knick-knack on the table: "Yes, in Naples."

These words were said so slowly and with such obvious hesitation that Hedwige began to tremble. "Has he changed his address?" she asked.

"Oh!" cried Mme Pauque softly. "What a strange question, but it goes straight to the heart of the subject. However, there's something improper in playing riddles under the present circumstances. I must tell you, my child, that you will never see him again."

"I will never see Jean again?"

"No," replied Mme Pauque firmly. "He lies at present in Italian soil. Hedwige, you don't seem to understand: Jean is dead."

Hedwige rose to her feet: "My letter," she whispered.

"What was that?" asked Mme Pauque. "Sit down, my child. Jean did not hold a very large place in our hearts, but I can imagine how much this news upsets you."

Hedwige walked across the room one way, then the other.

"Dead," she said.

"Yes," replied Mme Pauque, also rising. "He was only forty, but a man without much of a future. One couldn't imagine his future, which is always a bad sign."

She walked about a little and stopped under the chandelier, whose crystals shone like drops of water.

"How did he die?" asked Hedwige at last.

"Didn't you hear what Raoul said a few minutes ago? He talked about a stupid accident. No? That was the stupid accident. Accidents are always termed stupid in such cases, and yet . . ." Her hands opened and closed. "I think you should go up to your room," she said, confidentially. "You'll sleep, tonight."

Mme Pauque was not mistaken. Hedwige went to bed almost immediately and dropped into a heavy sleep interspersed with long dreams that followed each other closely and confusedly but in which Gaston Dolange always appeared. Sometimes he plunged into the river and came out with dripping, golden limbs, and a laugh that terrified Hedwige, and she was also afraid that if he took her in his arms he would soil her dress, but he handed her a letter, then another and yet another, and all these letters disappeared like birds in flight. Suddenly, he rushed up to her with a knife that was long and bloodstained to the hilt. She woke gasping, and called Ulrique in a strangled voice.

Midnight struck. She went to sleep almost at once, and there he was again. He was dressed, this time, and laughed as he showed her something that she could not see. "Here, now look, here," he said. But she did not know what he meant, she could see nothing; then he threw her on the ground, put his arms around her neck, and Mme Pauque's voice whispered: "Accidents are always termed stupid in such cases. . . ." At that moment, Hedwige felt that the ground opened gently under her body and that she slipped into a hole that was exactly her length. She tried to move unsuccessfully. Her shrieks of terror woke her as daylight appeared through the shutters and marked the carpet with yellow stripes.

Her first thought was for the letter that she had written Jean. It would probably be sent back to her, as she had written her address on the back of the envelope, but the idea that it might fall into Mme Pauque's hands sickened her, and she decided, from then on, to watch for the delivery of every mail. How much she regretted having allowed herself to be drawn into confidences, and above all, to have asked Jean to arrange for her to meet Gaston Dolange again! She had called on a dead man for help. A dead man . . . These words had little meaning for her, as she had never seen anyone dead, and it seemed unimaginable that Jean should no longer be alive. He had been absent, a short time ago. He continued to be absent now. He was simply a long way off.

The letter did not return. Hedwige wandered about the house without leaving it, for four days, dreading that someone might intercept her mail. She pretended to have headaches which were put down to emotion. Once or twice Mme Vasseur tried to make her go out with her, but was not too pressing, for Hedwige's company bored her. As to Mme Pauque, she kept a deep silence and almost always happened on Hedwige, as she returned from the concierge's lodge. And almost unconsciously, the two women engaged in a kind of game which consisted in causing or avoiding encounters of such a trifling nature that, in an ordinary way, they would never have been noticed. They smiled without exchanging a word when they chanced to meet, and Mme Pauque looked down at the girl's hands while Hedwige looked up at pallid, symmetrical features that were completely expressionless.

One evening, a servant handed a letter to Hedwige; she took it from the silver tray with an eagerness that she immediately regretted not having better concealed, for she saw a smile in Herbert's eyes and, feeling suspicious, turned to see Mme Pauque coming up to her. There was a moment of hesitation, then Hedwige glanced at the envelope and recognized the big, arrogant handwriting.

"Ulrique," she remarked simply.

"I know," said Mme Pauque, going past her, "Ulrique is coming back."

The letter, in fact, said little else.

"I will be home Sunday," wrote Ulrique. *"Ask Berthe to take my blue suit out of its bag and air it. I don't want to smell of moth balls. Remind me to tell you about two things."*

That was all. The short note was not signed, and it went without saying that when Hedwige would ask her cousin what were the two things she was to be told, the answer would be a shrug: "If you think I can remember!"

Hedwige remained motionless, holding the envelope. Ulrique's return upset her. She had often appealed to her, mentally, but she thought that she had gone away for a very long time, and now the idea that her cousin would be home in a couple of days disturbed her greatly, because at present everything was quite different. Everything? What did everything mean? Perhaps it meant that everything within her had changed.

That night, she decided to call on the antique dealer the next afternoon. The fact was that when Ulrique returned, such a thing would be far more difficult, but tomorrow, between the two last mails, she could go out for an hour. The house was empty, around six o'clock. M. Vasseur and Raoul had not returned from their offices, and as for Mme Vasseur and her sister, they had been invited to a reception that would last until dinnertime.

Hedwige always felt comforted when she made a decision, no matter what it was. She then had moments of extreme rapture and her heart grew lighter, as though a miracle had taken place. And what would she say to Arlette? That, she did not yet know. She would be guided by inspiration, at the very last moment. The important thing was to act. "To act," she said to herself aloud, in her silent bedroom, as she looked at herself in the mirror with a hard, stern face. She stared at herself for a moment and said more loudly: "I must act, or die."

Such words had a strange resonance at an hour when everyone was asleep, and she repeated them with even greater pleasure than she had had the first time. So, while other people rested in their beds, she was awake, her hair over her shoulders, saying to that woman in the mirror that she must act or die, and she said it to night, to silence, to solitude, and she could not help thinking she looked beautiful at a moment when words fraught with such meaning parted her lips.

The next day, at about half-past six, she ran to the antique dealer. Arlette was about to close her shop and greeted her visitor with exclamations of joy.

"You! What a surprise! I dared not write, but I've been thinking about you. Ah! no, we aren't going to stay here! This time, I'll take you up to my flat."

After locking the door, she directed Hedwige to the winding staircase which led to a dark, cozy little apartment. Shutters tempered the warmth of the setting sun and, on a large Persian rug, narrow strips of light set the bright colors of the wool ablaze; big orange flowers stood out against a dark ground, arresting attention and holding it spellbound.

"Lovely, isn't it?" asked Arlette, following Hedwige's admiring glance. "I paid four thousand francs for it last year. It's worth five at present. Let's sit down, my little Hedwige."

Seizing her hand, she sat very close to Hedwige on a large Régence settee covered in shot silk. By degrees, the furniture became visible in the dusky light. A bouquet of red roses stood on a table with delicately curved legs, and filled the room with its melancholy fragrance.

"Shall I turn on the light?" asked Arlette, jingling the bracelets that slid over her arms. "No, you wouldn't care for it? It's the prettiest time of the day. . . . I'll get you a drink."

"Thank you," said Hedwige, "nothing for me."

She wanted to draw away a little, for she did not like anyone to touch her, and Arlette sat far too close, but the cushions were so deep and soft that it was difficult to move. All of a sudden, she laid her fist over her heart and whispered:

"I have something to say to you."

"Something to say to me," said Arlette, turning

little, animal eyes toward her. "Oh! How moved she is! Speak, my child."

"I want the address of . . . you know who. . . ."

The sentence fell into a deep silence, then the dealer grasped Hedwige's hand and murmured:

"My poor child! I knew it. When I saw you standing in the shop, with that tragic expression . . . Listen to me. We're going to talk together like two old friends. I see only too well that you completely misunderstand the young man in question, but you're in love, and love is something that can't be argued. You want to write to him, eh? That's not the thing to do. To begin with, a letter is something tangible and you never can tell what it might become in the hands of a lad like young Dolange." Hedwige made a gesture. "Oh! Don't be annoyed. If you want to write to him, it's because you want to see him, and if you want to see him, well, you shall. Arlette will take care of that. You shall see him here, in this very room. Aren't you glad?"

Hedwige looked at her without a word, but tears rolled down her cheeks.

"Come now," continued Arlette in a lower voice, "we're crying, but those are tears of joy, aren't they? I can't say I believe in miracles where such a young man is concerned, but I wonder, seeing that you're so pretty, I wonder . . ."

"I'm not very pretty," said Hedwige, bursting into sobs.

Arlette's arms closed on her, as on so much booty.

"Weep," she said, "weep on Arlette's bosom. It will do you good, and it won't be the first time that I've comforted girls like you, but I'm sorry for you, little Hedwige. How well you've chosen your tormentor! However, I'll tell you what to do. You two shall meet.

in this corner. The sights this room has seen! Ah! If it could only talk, ha, ha!"

She laughed suddenly and hugged a struggling Hedwige with all her strength. Brusquely, they parted, gasping a little, and Hedwige blew her nose.

"How upset we are, the pair of us," said Arlette running her fingers through her hair. "And I feel so sorry for you. I see only too clearly all the mistakes you're going to make—and I want to help you."

The room grew shadowy then, and Hedwige's voice whispered:

"Do you promise that I'll see him here?"

"I promise," said Arlette with theatrical good nature. "That young Dolange of yours would walk across the whole town just to have a drink. It might open your eyes to talk with him a little, perhaps."

"And when shall I see him?"

"Give me three days' time. I'll drop you a note."

"Three days!" cried Hedwige despairingly.

"Well, come back day after tomorrow. I'll tell him I have a surprise for him. That always works."

"Oh," said Hedwige, "it would be better not to talk about a surprise."

"Poor little thing! She's afraid he might be disappointed. But you can make yourself easy on that point: you won't be the surprise."

Hedwige blushed in the dark, was about to ask a question, but held her tongue.

"What's to be understood as a surprise," muttered Arlette, "is not in the least what you imagine. If I knew where to reach him, I'd call him up, but at this time of day . . ."

"What did you say?" asked Hedwige.

"Nothing. I was thinking aloud. You'll see him, never fear, but . . . Oh, maybe I shouldn't say this. It's about our dear Ulrique. . . . She promised to ask me to your house—why, the very day of the reception at which you met Gaston Dolange. Need I tell you that she didn't invite me? I was a little vexed with her on that account, not much, because you can't be vexed for long with such a beautiful woman, but if you could . . ."

"If I could?"

Arlette leaned toward her and whispered in her ear:

"If you could ask Mme Vasseur to invite me to her house! There! I've let it out," she added, squeezing Hedwige's hand. "Oh! Don't think I'm bargaining with you. You'll see that pretty young fellow of yours, but everything would be on a better footing if I were received by your family . . . once. You see, it would improve my standing with my customers."

"Yes," said Hedwige. "I'll try."

"I'll try isn't enough for me," replied Arlette in a falsely playful voice. "What would you think if I said that *I would try* to have you meet young Dolange again?"

"Oh! I promise to!" cried Hedwige.

Arlette burst out laughing.

"You and I get on so well together," she said. "It's extraordinary that we should not have met before, but that's Ulrique's fault. By the way, you're not to say a word to Ulrique about our little plot. We had better take advantage of her being away."

"I won't breathe a word of it, and I think that Ulrique should really not know about it. I'm afraid of Ulrique. . . . Anyway, I don't know why I say this. She is so very nice. . . ."

"Nice? Oh, certainly not!" cried Arlette. "Lovely, deep, mysterious as a mountain lake, attractive, yes. . . ."

Hedwige got up. "I must go," she said.

"Not yet," answered the dealer, pressing a button.

A small lamp with a pink shade gave such a gentle light that Hedwige was unaware that the shadowy room grew lighter.

"I haven't shown you my treasures," said Arlette, "what I call my treasures."

She rose and opened the drawer of a rococo console from which she took out an album before lighting another lamp that stood on the hinged leaf of a mahogany desk.

"Come here," she said.

Hedwige hesitated for an instant and obeyed. The antique dealer clasped the album to her breast.

"I'm not sure whether I should," she remarked. "And yet, I think so. My poor Hedwige, I could have introduced you to far prettier lads than young Dolange."

The album was suddenly laid on the desk flap and opened at the first page. The light shone full on a group of four photographs that were a little larger than postcards. At first, Hedwige did not understand, then her glance fell on the portrait of a young man who smiled with the greatest assurance. The one next him appeared more serious and wore an unbraided military *képi*. Hedwige raised her eyes to meet the dealer's attentive stare. Arlette began to smile and laid a finger with a ruby-red nail on one of the likenesses.

"This one," she whispered.

"What do you mean?" asked Hedwige. "Who is it? I don't know him."

"Of course you don't," said Arlette slowly, as she

closed the album, "but he's better-looking than young Dolange, and that one would have fallen in love with you. . . ."

Hedwige felt the blood rushing to her face and remained motionless, not knowing what to say.

"We'll find you a sweetheart," whispered Arlette at last, and Hedwige felt her breath on her neck.

After a moment of uncertainty, Hedwige stretched out her hand as though she wanted to drive something away. She had felt frightened for a little while, without knowing why, and did not know how to leave a room where everything suddenly appeared to be so mysterious.

"No," she said.

With a violent effort, she managed to reach the door and turned to Arlette, who smiled at her, motionless.

"So I'm to come back day after tomorrow?" asked Hedwige rather hoarsely.

"Day after tomorrow," replied Arlette gently. Walking ahead of Hedwige, she led her to the stairs. A few seconds later, Hedwige was out of the shop and in the street.

She woke with a start at dawn: there was someone in the room, she was sure of it, a man hid behind the curtains, and her heart began to thump in her breast while she heard the hiss of terror in her ears. Her panic-stricken hand fumbled for the switch of her bedside lamp and suddenly the room appeared. No one was there. A bird sang in the big linden in the courtyard and the air smelt good. She tried to remember her dream and could not quite succeed. The room looked as usual, although it had the somewhat curious aspect of places that are dragged out of the darkness where they have been fast asleep, like living beings. Obviously, no one hid behind the curtains; there would not have been room enough, but Hedwige once more was terrified at the idea that they might part to let someone come into the room, because that, and that only, remained in her mind of a strange dream, more real and far more disturbing than reality. She gradually calmed down and, with a kind of gratitude, let her eyes wander around her. The walls, furniture, banal engravings, everything told her not to be afraid.

She lay back in bed but did not turn out the light and went to sleep at once. In her dreams, she saw a humbly dressed man who smiled at her silently. Hours went by, it seemed, then the stranger came close to the bed, leaned over Hedwige, and tenderly laid his hand on her forehead. She cried and woke up in tears.

Her first thought was for the next day: in a little more than twenty-four hours, she would see Gaston Dolange again, but life had to be endured till then, the moment when they were to meet must be reached, as an inmense space is crossed to attain an objective. Breakfasting, washing, talking to one and another, that meant travelling toward an occasion that she dreaded and longed for at the same time, that meant going to the dimly lit room where the antique dealer had shown her the album. How much like a dream had everything seemed since the last few days! Life no longer appeared real, or it appeared real in a different manner. Hedwige remembered Arlette's cryptic smile as she opened that album of photographs. And that blood-colored fingernail laid below the smiling young man's face. Hedwige dreaded that Ulrique should hear about all this, but Ulrique would not be back for two days and

Arlette would not speak, because Arlette was afraid of Ulrique.

Her mind filled with these things, she left her room a little later and was about to go down the oaken staircase when a hum of voices followed by a muffled noise stopped her at the top of the steps. She turned instinctively. The sound came from another part of the house and was succeeded by deep silence. Hedwige hesitated and then, instead of going down, returned to her room and left it through another door that opened on a long passage with walls hung in red linen. By going in that direction, and making a detour through a small library where no one ever set foot, you reached the grand staircase whose pale gray marble steps spread proudly around their axis like a large fan held by an invisible thumb.

Hedwige crossed the landing and stopped motionless, her hand on the wrought-iron stair rail. At the very bottom of the stairs, less than a yard from the large, glazed front door, lay something black. She held her breath. It was a trunk, a kind of long, narrow chest fitted with two iron handles. In the cheerful light of that April morning, sunbeams lightly touching the white walls, the trunk gave an impression of dreadful sadness that no words could convey, for it spoke of solitude and despair in the mute language of things which is not the language of human beings.

One glance was enough for Hedwige to realize what it was. It's Jean's trunk, she thought, and moving back, she murmured a sentence that she herself scarcely heard:

"He is dead."

It struck her like a revelation. She could not keep her

eyes from the wooden chest, for a bond existed between herself and this object, a very strong bond, she felt with horror, and her impression was that the trunk attempted to convey a message to her.

A door opened and made her start. She took refuge in the little library and from there heard Mme Vasseur's dry voice giving orders. At the same instant, Hedwige's legs gave way and she dropped to the floor without uttering a sound. Darkness swept over her like a sheet.

When she came to, she wondered what had happened to her and trembled at the thought that she might have been seen lying at the foot of a long writing table, for the library door had remained ajar, but people rarely went into that part of the house, and she ran back to her own room.

The day passed quietly, as usual. The two men went to their offices, Mme Vasseur and her sister left the house in the afternoon, each bent on a round of calls. The trunk was not mentioned, and disappeared almost at once. Hedwige felt tempted to inquire about it at lunch, but an entirely different subject was discussed and she dared not ask the question that could be read in her eyes. It seemed to her that she need only say: "Where is the black trunk?" for this funereal object to appear suddenly in the middle of the table; but conversation turned on a rather risqué play, which was to be performed by a Parisian company during the following month, at the finest theater in town. Mme Vasseur declared that this would be a great event and wondered if it would be possible to be seen at the play on the first night. Of course, there were screened boxes for those who wished to see without being seen, but these seats were most uncomfortable.

"If the play raises a scandal," said Raoul, "I don't wish it to be said that we were seen there."

"Wait for the play to be reviewed," said M. Vasseur. "Critics will set the lead. You can go later."

"Yes, but the first performance!" cried Mme Vasseur. "The first night will be the most interesting one."

They argued about the play until coffeetime, but Hedwige no longer listened. She saw the trunk in place of the epergne of red flowers, and in the trunk was her letter. Had the trunk been opened? Had her letter been found? No one said a word about all this. The conversation would have been no different if the trunk had never been set down at the foot of the staircase. Hedwige wondered whether she had not imagined it all, and for a moment took refuge in the thought, as though it were a shelter against unhappiness. However, it was unreasonable to believe that she had not seen what her memory pictured with such faithful precision, and, passing from one extreme to the other, once more she imagined the trunk to be on the table, but of a far greater length, and in this chest was Jean, and in Jean's hand was the letter she had written him. A little cry of distress rose to her lips. Four heads turned to her.

"What's the matter, my child?" asked Mme Pauque.

Hedwige blushed without answering.

"She doesn't go out enough," said Raoul. "When Ulrique comes home, I'll tell her to look after her."

"Don't you feel well?" asked Mme Vasseur.

"Oh, yes, perfectly well," replied Hedwige. "I don't know why I cried out. I was thinking of something."

"She was thinking of something," repeated Raoul with a knowing smile.

Once she was alone in the house, Hedwige went up

to her room and walked through it to go down the passage—the one hung in red linen—again. Like a child, but a child that played in good earnest, she tried her best to believe in the impossible: it was not really four in the afternoon, but ten in the morning, and she was going toward the grand staircase because she had just heard a noise coming from that direction, she passed through the little library, she advanced, and now she stood on the marble landing and laid her hand on the wrought-iron stair rail, eyes closed, heart thumping. If the trunk was there . . . But how could such ideas flit through her mind? She opened her eyes: there was nothing, nothing but the large, worn flagstones, but she looked at the spot where she had seen the trunk and felt that if she stayed there long enough, she would end by seeing it once more.

Seized with fear suddenly, she went back to her room for shelter. What to do? At times it seemed of utmost importance to recover possession of her letter, and at others a matter of indifference. She did not care if the whole town knew that she was in love with Gaston Dolange and that she had begged the unfortunate Jean to arrange for her to meet the young man again. A little more than twenty-four hours divided her from the moment when she would see him again. The idea filled her with rapture. Then she imagined Raoul reading certain sentences in her letter and reddened with anger.

The trunk had probably been taken up to Jean's room. She tiptoed up to the top story. The servants were in the pantry, at that hour; she ran no risk of being observed but was careful, however, to be very quiet and walked down the passage leading to the room that Jean would never see again. The door was at the end of the passage, painted gray, with an olive-shaped brass knob.

Deep silence reigned in this part of the house, and Hedwige had the impression that the whole dwelling came alive and was observant. She stretched out her hand, turned the knob in her fist, right, then left. The door was locked.

Hedwige waited a few seconds, then tried once more to open the door. The sound of the knob as it turned filled the silence, but the door held fast. Then she called Jean in a whisper.

The dead man's name struck the air, went through the thickness of the panel, wandered through the empty little room where he had lived. Hedwige started and looked around her. If anyone had heard her, she would have been taken for a lunatic, but there was no one in the passage. Through a fanlight above her head, she saw the pale blue sky and across it sailed tattered clouds, like pieces of torn white lace. Never before had she experienced such deep loneliness. Leaning her head against the door, she allowed herself to drift away once more on the current of her habitual thoughts, and, rather than call up a dead man, she mentally called up the living one who made her suffer. She fancied him to be the door and kissed it again and again, laying her lips on the wooden surface with a kind of furious, desperate tenderness.

Some time after, she went away, sad and ashamed, and walked down to her bedroom on the next floor. It struck her suddenly that her letter was not in Jean's room, but somewhere else in the house: that appeared to her as an unquestionable and obvious fact. The trunk had been opened, the letter removed. Everybody would be back in a little less than two hours. She resolved to take advantage of whatever time was left to explore a few drawers.

The first room she went to was Mme Pauque's. Walls papered in dull gray tinged with mauve, purple velvet curtains at the windows, it presented an indefinable aspect of austerity and fastidiousness. A bouquet of white roses blooming in a crystal urn scented the air, and was the first object to attract attention. In an angle of the room, an Empire dressing table, severely straight but provided with a great number of brushes, combs, bottles, and boxes of cosmetics, testified to the care that Mme Pauque took of her person and also to the good opinion that she had of her outward appearance. A plain mahogany bed, grave and narrow, spoke of sound sleep, and repelled, with a kind of mute violence, any idea of voluptuousness. Hedwige noticed a small photograph on the mantelpiece, half concealed by the foot of a silver candlestick, that reproduced the features of the deceased M. Pauque, a handsome, well-fed man, but whose likeness was yellowing.

It frightened Hedwige a little to be in this room, and she thought that she would drop dead if Mme Pauque suddenly put in an appearance, but she knew that she had nothing to fear as Mme Pauque had gone out with Mme Vasseur. A highboy by the window presented its polished surface to the light and, in certain places, looked like tortoise shell, but each one of its seven drawers was locked and resisted Hedwige's efforts, so she directed her attention to another part of the room.

At the head of the bed, a small door covered in the same paper as the walls was almost invisible, yet a cut-glass knob betrayed it, all the more since a sunbeam struck this object and turned it into a diamond. Hedwige remembered a hanging closet where Mme Pauque kept her clothes and, seized with sudden curiosity, crossed the room breadthways. She would not, to be sure, find her letter in a cupboard, but then she had only seen this dark, roomy closet two or three times in her life, and it was connected in her mind with ghost stories; the desire to cast an eye over it was so strong that it made her forget her other worries for the time being. And then, it would have been absurd to feel frightened in the lovely light of afternoon.

She turned the knob and the door opened. Hedwige saw nothing, at first, but smelt a light, agreeable odor that seemed made up of twenty different perfumes, and as her eyes grew accustomed to the darkness she discerned her aunt's dresses, hanging in perfect order and completely motionless. It was this immobility that struck Hedwige, for she remembered that as a child she fancied that all these dresses moved a little, if you looked at them long enough, and that a hand, then a face appeared between the folds of material; and recalling her terror, she shuddered involuntarily.

Taking a step forward, she stumbled over something and could not keep from crying out. She pushed the clothes aside slightly to see better, thrust her arm in. All of a sudden, she had a lump in her throat and in her ears the almost imperceptible hissing noise which, for her, was a sign of fear: at her feet, sure enough, she recognized Jean's trunk.

For a few seconds she remained bent, dazed by this discovery, and suddenly she realized that drops of sweat ran down her forehead to her cheeks. Straightening up with an effort, she backed out of the closet and closed the door by pushing it to with both hands. She shook from head to foot. For a moment she looked at the sunbeam that showed her the cut-glass knob, and the whole room seemed decked with funereal majesty, in the peaceful stillness of the afternoon.

She went out, almost at a run, and sat on the stairs until she recovered; finally, her mind grew calmer and she thought her fright ridiculous. Yet, she did not return to Mme Pauque's room but walked up a flight to visit Mme Vasseur's: a huge, disorderly apartment, with clothes flung on the bed and over the backs of armchairs, with bottles of toilet water cluttering up the mantelpiece and milliners' bandboxes obstructing the way between pieces of furniture. Hedwige opened the drawers of a commode and closed them in discouragement: it was only too clear that the letter was not to be found there. "It's in the trunk," said a voice inside her head.

"No," said Hedwige aloud.

She walked down a passage and entered Raoul's room. Here, within walls papered in pink with a red stripe, triumphed the most virile neatness and banality. Stiff armchairs suggested a seated position rather than a temptation to rest. Above the brass bed hung a diploma together with photographs of relatives and a general view of ironworks. A desk with a closed hinged leaf, a bedside table, that was all. Not a book. Hedwige's expression was heavy with sadness as she looked around her. If Raoul had laid hands on the wretched letter, it must be hidden in the desk, and that was locked, obviously. Which drawer was she to search? There were no drawers. Yes, there was one. The little bedside table had a drawer with a brass knob. Hedwige opened it.

The drawer made a kind of whispering as it slipped through its grooves, and Hedwige saw nothing at first but a package of tobacco and a box of matches, then, at the very back, something shining. She hesitated for an instant, once more with the strange feeling that the whole house watched her every movement attentively.

Finally, she stretched out a finger and touched a metallic object. She knew at once that it was Raoul's revolver. It so happened that Ulrique had talked to Hedwige more than once about this weapon, one that its owner would never have dreamt of putting under lock and key, any more than he would have locked up his pipe or razor. Ulrique explained to her cousin, with a contemptuous laugh, that for Raoul the revolver replaced the courage he lacked, for the brusque, blustering little man was frightened. "Note that he'd never dare use it," she added in her sibilant voice, "but the gun reassures him."

These words came back to Hedwige, and she picked up the revolver to examine it more closely. Her hand shook a little, but she had a weird sensation as she fingered a dangerous object, one that spoke of death. It was smaller than she would have thought, colder, less heavy. Her finger barely touched the trigger, and with a shiver of horror and pleasure she pointed the barrel mouth at her face. Almost a minute passed before she could bring herself to turn the small, brutally shaped, and wicked object aside, then, the strangeness of her attitude filled her with sudden dread and she replaced the weapon at the back of the drawer.

The clock in the drawing room struck five. Hedwige heard the strokes through the floor. The faint, reedy little noise brought her back to everyday life and she felt secretly grateful to it, but almost immediately she thought: He doesn't love me, and her eyes filled with tears. What meaning could there be to living on this earth if she was not loved? What use were her arms, her head, her feet? What sense was there in the beating of a heart, the ceaseless work of lungs drawing in air and driving it out again? Her body was her own self.

She was those useless hands, with their delicate skin and, under their skin, blood and bones. What on earth could all that mean? She had no idea what to do with the whole of her being as it moved about in space, suffering. To go here, stay there, no longer had a meaning. She should have been nowhere, as she was not loved.

She left the room and began to wander aimlessly through the house. Life went by. That was the most important thing. That life should go by until she saw Gaston Dolange, and that everything should remain motionless then: minutes, seconds, time. She entered the little library at random, the room where she had fainted that morning, and, looking at rows of books whose somber binding darkened the room, she thought: How many things are indifferent to me!

A sudden whim made her stretch out on the floor, on the spot where she had fallen unconscious, a few hours before. In this position she could see, under a flat kneehole writing table, the contorted feet of this elegant piece of furniture, and as she lay there she longed to die and envied Jean, who slept under the ground, at Naples, and tried to imagine that she herself was dead, closing her eyes, holding her breath. If she really died, she would be found, lying like that. And what would he say when he heard that she was dead?

She rose and went to the grand staircase. Just as she had that morning, as she had a moment ago, she leaned against the ironwork and looked down the steps. Nothing was there. The trunk was in Mme Pauque's closet, and in the trunk was her letter.

"No, it isn't," she said aloud.

Once again, she thought of Jean. She remembered a nurse she had had as a little girl, who talked to her once about a woman who had just died. Hedwige did not know what death was. She asked: "Dead? What's going to happen to her?" "Oh!" the nurse replied, "they'll put her in a box and take her away." This sentence had terrified Hedwige to such a point that she still thought of it with childish anxiety, and it was on account of that sentence that she had been frightened in the closet, although she had not dared own it to herself. She was ashamed. She knew very well that the dead man had not been put into that trunk, and yet, after a certain fashion, he was in it: his clothes were there, his shoes, his old black hat. That was why she had run away.

A moment later, she entered M. Vasseur's room, less in the hope of finding her letter than to help time pass more quickly, but as she had the feeling of being indiscreet, she hesitated on the threshold. The room was small, with a window on a deserted street, and presented a gloomy, unpretentious aspect; there was nothing there to arouse curiosity. The oak furniture, which came straight from a department store, was patterned on what was then called the modern style and formed great masses of shadow that suggested a shipwreck. On the bedside table with a white marble top, an alarm clock filled the silence with its flat, hollow ticking; there was something inexorable about the sound, much like the step of a traveller bent on reaching his objective. The paper on the walls was blue and black with geometrical designs both violent and complicated that teased and disturbed the eye. It required a saint or a brute to live peacefully in such an infernally commonplace setting, but M. Vasseur was neither one nor the other; he had chosen both wallpaper and furniture in all innocence, like a man who did not see what lay before him.

Hedwige hated this room; its ugliness gave her a feeling of uneasiness that the sunlight streaming in at the window could not dispel, and she stood, undecided, for a minute or so, on the atrocious multi-colored rug. It would have seemed shameful to her to rummage in M. Vasseur's drawers, for she was too keenly aware that this good and simple man grieved to see her unhappy and was fond of her. She sighed, after a time, and was about to leave the room when she noticed a black cross, the size of a little finger, hanging above the bed on the wall and hidden among lightning-shaped stripes.

Astonishment prevented her from moving, and she stood perfectly still as though she had seen a ghost. Religion was never discussed in the Vasseurs' house. Hedwige herself had grown up in unbelief and passed by churches as one walks by law courts or any other monument in which one is pretty certain of never setting foot. To her eyes, the cross was part of a collection of things that one is used to seeing and about which no self-examination is necessary, because they are meaningless, excepting to others, but the presence of such an object in M. Vasseur's room was something that she could not understand. I didn't know he had such views, she thought. Then, thinking it over for a few seconds, she told herself that the cross was probably an heirloom and left the room as she had left the others.

Something that she could not quite make out disturbed her. Hanging on the zigzag-patterned wallpaper, the black cross had given her a shock. Perhaps it was bad luck to happen suddenly on a cross. . . . She saw herself once more in the park sitting on a bench by Mme Pauque, who read her Jean's letter, and fragments of sentences came back to her: ". . . If I had greater faith . . . I am hated for being the way that God created me. . . ." What did all that mean? The letter had been torn up and thrown into the sewer ("That's the proper place for it," Mme Pauque had said). Where was it at present? In the river, very far from the town. And Jean? Jean was buried in the ground. How deep? Under how many feet of horrible black earth, full of worms, were the dead hidden? ". . . the way that God created me. . . ." So he believed in such things. She remembered that Ulrique had once talked to her about this, but in an absent-minded and contemptuous manner, because Jean's beliefs interested neither one of them.

Following a passage, she walked by Ulrique's room and slackened her pace a little, then stopped. There was no reason to enter Ulrique's room, if it meant going there to look for the letter she had written Jean, and also, even though she was away, Hedwige was frightened of her cousin. "I forbid anyone to enter my room!" Hedwige was familiar with that sentence from having heard it ring through the house at times when, as Mme Vasseur expressed it, Ulrique declared war on the world. "I forbid you . . ." Hedwige could hear Ulrique's stormy voice shrieking the words at her. Hesitant, she reflected for a whole minute, turned back, and suddenly grasped the doorknob. No . . . Dared she? She turned the knob violently, but the door did not open. When Ulrique said no, it meant no, and Hedwige blushed as though her face had been slapped. Then a furious longing possessed her to force her way into the room. This she wanted to do because she was dying of boredom. How exciting it would have been, and what a relief if she could have talked to Ulrique in a room where something of her personality lingered. She would have held forth, delivered the long speech that her head and heart imprisoned and that was ready to rush out, the speech of terror, the loud appeal for help. She did not want to sink like a stone, drown without crying out. Her heart thumped. She struck the door with her fist. What she could never have told Ulrique if she had been present she could so easily have told an absent, mute, yet attentive Ulrique, an ideal, *human* Ulrique. . . .

Her desire to enter the room was so strong that she suddenly had the delusion of crossing the threshold of this inviolate apartment, and, eyes shut, forehead close to the door panel, she saw herself standing in the middle of the room.

To her right stood a vast bed fancifully designed and much too large for one person, but Ulrique slept diagonally. "I need a lot of room," she said in her queenly manner. And she added, to Hedwige's embarrassment, as it sounded indecent: "No matter whether I'm on my back or my stomach, I sleep as though I'd been quartered." Why did she have to say such things? Yet, that was how she expressed it, looking defiant and her long jade cigarette holder between her fingers, and Hedwige mentally recoiled from her. . . .

To her left, the large pale blue silk armchair in which Ulrique lolled. "You sink into it as though it were a cloud," she said, "you can roll about in it like an animal. Just try it. . . ." But Hedwige preferred a chair. Snatches of conversation came back to her. What Ulrique said was not always very clear. She was fond of alluding to people whom Hedwige did not know: the Soudrys, the Andreanus, the whole of an elegant and mysterious crowd that had a good time on the outskirts of town. "They smoke," Ulrique would laconically reply to Hedwige's questions. Did they have to go such a long way just to smoke? This remark caused fits of laughter, for what Ulrique called her cousin's innocence was a source of mirth to the young woman in her gloomiest moments.

Ulrique, thought Hedwige, you who have everything in the world that you can wish, help me who have nothing of what I long for.

She leaned her head a little closer to the door and whispered: "Do something about it. . . ."

In the room where she imagined that she stood, the walls were almost completely hidden under innumerable photographs of pictures that celebrated physical beauty, and on the mantelpiece a curly-headed Greek god stared blindly at the door.

Hedwige suddenly experienced a great emptiness inside her head and came back to herself. Steps sounding in her direction made her start; she ran away.

Once more in her room, once more in a shelter that became a prison after a few hours, and where she stared at the furniture, eyes heavy with boredom. How she hated the dressing table and its mirror that never reflected anything but the same little worried face! In spite of this, time had passed. She heard people coming and going in the house; there was one less afternoon in her life.

Her eyes fell on the alarm clock by her bed, and she could not check a gesture of alarm: it was past the mail hour. At the same instant she heard an almost imperceptible noise coming from the door and saw an envelope being gently slipped inside the room. She was at the door in a leap and opened it. Mme Pauque stood before her, smiling and lovely in the daylight that played on her unwrinkled face.

"I should have given you this letter sooner," she said,

calling her attention to the envelope at their feet with a glance. "It came this morning, registered. We looked for you. Perhaps you were out."

"I was in the library," replied Hedwige, bending to pick up the envelope.

Mme Pauque was going downstairs with her rapid, almost noiseless step when Hedwige stood upright. The girl's eyes followed the graceful figure, then she closed the door and examined the envelope. Her hand shook a little. The letter was from Jean. Sitting on her bed, she opened the letter and began to read it:

"My little Hedwige, this letter will reach you when everything in this world will be over for me. I am leaving it. You will be told of an accident, because you are young and should be gently dealt with, but I have always tried to tell you the truth, I have always wanted to tell someone the truth before going. There has not been an accident. I want to go, to anticipate my time, too slow in coming. Tonight, the poison that I keep in a drawer will bring peace to my body, if I have courage enough to do a very simple thing. Otherwise, if I'm afraid of my soul, this letter, that you will receive nevertheless, will make me look very ridiculous in your eyes, but I believe and hope that I will not flinch.

"I feel, in writing you this letter, that I am doing you a great deal of harm, and yet I must go on with it, even if I make you suffer more keenly, for I am very fond of you and want you to live, though I must die. I am intensely sorry for you. I don't know whether I can tell you why. See how lacking I am in greatness, on the threshold of death! I have such a respect for you that it seems impossible to me to commit to paper certain sentences that might perhaps set you free by depriving you

of cruel hopes. I should speak, Hedwige, and I feel that I will not be equal to it. If you can believe me without asking yourself any questions, you will be safe from danger. This is difficult, but possible. Someday you must meet a man who will love you. You think, perhaps, that this does not depend on you, but there is something that weighs over your life, something which I do not scruple to call a curse, and I want you to escape it, because you are young and should live.

"I am going to talk to you once more about the man who fills your mind and whose name I cannot bring myself to write. You should never have met him, and if you were brought face to face with him, it is no one's fault but your cousin Ulrique's. She knew only too well what she was doing when she introduced you to a young man whose face, alas, is so attractive, but whose heart is inaccessible to human tenderness. Without having any proofs of this, I feel convinced that your cousin wished to see what would happen, for she is a prey to boredom and almost all her evil deeds are actuated by the fact that she cannot be happy herself. And it also amused her to make someone else suffer, another person even more deeply in love with this young man than you are. A great deal could be said on the subject, and I will refrain. You unconsciously passed by a tragedy that bore a singular resemblance to yours: a tragedy that concerned a terrible defeat suffered by love and the unbearable, searing burn with which the memory of a human being marks the soul, but you could not see that, you were too ignorant of life and already fascinated by eyes that can never look at you with anything but icy indifference.

"Don't see him again, Hedwige. I want these to be the

last words I say to anyone on this earth. If life is no longer possible to me, may it, at least, be possible for you."

A wide space followed these lines, and at the very end of the paper was Jean's name, but the letters were so hastily formed that Hedwige had difficulty in recognizing the signature. She sat there for a long time, incapable of movement, the letter spread out on her knees, eyes riveted to rows of words that danced up and down before her. The idea slowly took shape in her mind that this message came to her from the world beyond the grave, and, getting up suddenly, she let the paper slip to the floor, then placed her foot on it. The sound of a door closing on the first floor made her start. Picking up the letter, she tore it into tiny pieces and threw it into the wastepaper basket; it was only a little later, as she washed her hands, that she realized that she was trembling.

Chapter 5

Now she found herself once more in Arlette's drawing room, and in the big, dark, low-ceilinged room once more she breathed in the scent of roses that took her back to the gardens of her childhood. The air was close and a stormy light filtered through the half-closed shutters. The first drops of rain already pattered on the window sills.

"You're a few minutes early," said Arlette in the rich, caressing voice she used to sell a questionable piece of furniture. "Oh! Don't think I'm reproaching you, my darling, but it's the lady's place to be late. He should be here any time now. I'll detain him downstairs."

"Did he say he'd come?" asked Hedwige rather hoarsely.

Arlette gave a short little laugh.

"It's not for him to say he'll come," she said. "He just obeys. That kind of young man is easy enough to manage, but you have to know how. . . . I like your dress," she broke off suddenly. "That pale, rather indefinite shade of blue . . . Ulrique, of course?"

"Yes, Ulrique chose it for me."

"What taste she has. . . . Come now, don't look so flustered. You must behave a little coldly to young Dolange. You just chanced to drop in. I'll introduce you to each other as though you had never met, and his name must mean nothing to you. After a while, I'll leave you together, as though I had a customer to see. No nonsense, now! No impulsiveness. He has no more heart than this chest where I store away logs. Of course, I'll give him a little talk before bringing him upstairs. I'll prepare him for you, but you mustn't expect great things the first time you see him—or the second. . . . Well, you wanted to see him, didn't you? He'll be fairly well behaved. That, I can guarantee. Someday, I'll give him a few drinks. Not today. He turns nasty then and tells the truth, but later on, we'll see. I'll fix something up. Tell me, my little Hedwige, did you talk to Madame Vasseur about me?"

Hedwige blushed. "Yes," she said.

"Are you sure?"

"Why, yes, of course."

There was a silence, and the antique dealer stared straight at Hedwige, who rested her hand against the back of an armchair, in order not to fall, for her legs gave way slightly; she thought that all her hopes were about to collapse and continued in a voice she could scarcely recognize:

"I'll speak to her again this evening, I promise you. Anyway," she continued with sudden glibness, "she seems very well disposed toward you. She knows your shop, she admires . . ."

A bell rang discreetly on the ground floor, and Hedwige's sentence remained unfinished.

"I'm going downstairs," said Arlette slowly. "It's probably he. You realize that if I stayed up here with you he would go away, not seeing anyone about, and then it would be . . . a washout, wouldn't it?"

"I beg of you," whispered Hedwige.

"What day shall I drop in?"

"Next week. . . . Let's say next Thursday," said Hedwige.

By then, she thought, perhaps something will have happened. She dared not tell herself: Perhaps something will happen to this woman.

"There now," said Arlette, "I'll have pity on you. All the more since that little rascal of a Gaston is capable of bagging my Japanese curios. When I think that he was asked to your house, whereas I . . . Well!"

She gave a sudden start of indignation and left Hedwige to go down the winding staircase and vanish. Hedwige followed her with a beating heart to the top of the stairs and almost immediately heard Arlette greet someone facetiously. Hedwige strained her ear but at first could hear only a confused hum of conversation, as the antique dealer was now talking in another part of the shop. To hear better, it was necessary to walk down a step, then another, leaning against the stair rail, and go down yet farther at the risk of being seen.

"Why did I make you come here?" asked the antique dealer. "What questions you do ask! It makes you wonder who brought you up. Have you ever had to complain to me, tell me that, you blackguard?"

The last word was spoken in a suddenly affectionate voice.

"You said you had a surprise for me," said Gaston. "Where is it?"

"First, I must explain what it's all about."

Hedwige instinctively raised her hand to her throat. What it was all about—it was all about her, Hedwige. She was the surprise! Why didn't she die of shame? She was too perturbed at present to make out what Arlette and the young man said to each other, she no longer wanted to hear, and, going back to the drawing room, took shelter in the darkest corner, in the depths of a black velvet sofa whose cushions sank under her weight and softly pressed her around the waist and shoulders.

For a minute, she wondered whether she were not about to faint, for everything darkened around her, but fear of being ridiculous upheld her and gave her a certain courage. She did not want Arlette to find her in a faint: it would amuse her too much. . . . What a good time she would have telling her friends about it, the hypocrite! And Gaston Dolange? What would he think if he saw her in that condition, unconscious, head lolling back, like a victim? With an effort that brought her whole body into play, she rose, furious: the idea of inspiring pity in that man filled her with horror. She looked at herself in a mirror, powdered her face carefully, and waited.

They appeared, a moment later, first Arlette, at once offhand and affected, with a slightly vulgar air (for there was more than one Arlette, each according to circumstances), then, sulky and obstinate, with something mulish even in the way that he bent his brow, "young Dolange." Hedwige looked at him, bewildered. Was this the man she loved so madly? He seemed shorter than she had thought, heavier. She saw him differently in her memory, she saw him handsomer.

"How lucky that little rascal of a Gaston is!" trumpeted Arlette. "As it happens, he wanted to see you again. . . . It's just as though he had a feeling you were here, my darling. There's nothing like chance for arranging matters."

Hedwige turned her face away, ashamed of Arlette's coarseness and everything that was all too clear in this dreadful farce.

"You'll have to excuse me," said Arlette. "I must keep an eye on the shop. Gaston, you know where to find the port and cigarettes."

As she passed Hedwige to leave the room, the latter took her hand and said in an almost imperceptible whisper:

"Don't go!"

"You little fool," answered Arlette in the same low tone, "you've got to take your *chance!*"

She turned, looked at Gaston, and said under her breath:

"Just burn a little incense in the Chinese bowl . . . to create an atmosphere."

On the staircase, when she was almost out of sight, she burst out laughing suddenly and exclaimed:

"What muffs you look, the pair of you! But you're charming, you know. Hedwige, let me congratulate you again over your dress."

And she went down to the shop, humming.

There was a short silence. Hedwige sat down on the black sofa while the young man, one hand in a pocket and looking very bored, opened the drawers of a long Régence table. He was of middle height but broad-shouldered and gave a curious impression of strength and insolence, and his gestures were those of a child rather than a man's. He wore a well-cut, dark green suit and his butter-colored hair shone in the dusky light. Hedwige could see a disdainful profile, the short tilted nose, the thick pouting mouth, against the light. A pang went through her. She suddenly recaptured the emotion that she had felt on seeing this face for the first time, and it was as though she fell in love for the first time. "What a nuisance," he grumbled, angrily closing a drawer, "she only has the kind of cigarettes I hate. You don't happen to have an American cigarette?" He looked at her over his shoulder as he said this.

"I don't smoke," she murmured.

He slowly crossed the room and opened a little oak cupboard with door panels embossed with a big star, then she heard bottles clinking.

"Will you have some port?" he asked.

"No, thank you."

He filled a glass and came up to her.

"Her port is vile," he said, sitting in a large grandfather chair. "Arlette is so stingy."

This did not prevent the glass of port from being swallowed at one gulp and put down on a black lacquered table, then the young man stretched his left arm out and crooked it to glance at a gold watch shining on his wrist.

"You'll have to excuse me in five minutes," he said. "I have an appointment at the other end of town in half an hour."

"An appointment?" repeated Hedwige, unconscious of what she was saying.

Gaston smiled indulgently and did not reply. He leaned his head back slightly, let himself slip down deep into the armchair, and was about to swing one leg over the arm of his chair when he changed his mind. Hedwige looked at him with horror. She saw his white, swelling neck, his broad, smooth hands lying on the dark velvet, and felt defenseless against a man whose attitude of contempt drove her back to despair. There was no doubt in her mind, alas, that he was as attractive as she had first thought, for she would have wished to be mistaken. Half sprawling on his back, he looked taller and more powerful, and she dimly felt that he was flouting her.

"You don't happen to know where she's put her albums?" he asked suddenly.

"Her albums? Why, no."

"She doesn't always put them in the same place. You see, she's afraid someone will sneak her photographs. Hasn't she shown them to you?"

Hedwige shook her head.

"That's because she doesn't know you well enough, but if you asked her to . . . We've been together for a good five minutes," he added abruptly.

Hedwige did not answer. He clasped his hands behind his head and continued:

"She asked me to stay a quarter of an hour, but I've got to run away, on account of that appointment. Now I come to think of it, I don't see any sense in this business. Did you have anything to say to me?"

Hedwige left the sofa, took a few steps toward the young man, and was tempted to slap the insolent face that looked at her mockingly and with raised eyebrows, but she controlled herself and imagined anger blazing in his cheeks and eyes of a blue that verged on violet in the fading light: to lift her hand against the young man was impossible, and she stood motionless, ashamed and fascinated.

"I have nothing to say to you," she said at last.

"Neither have I," he answered with a faint drawl in which she recognized a vulgar plebeian accent, and this voice was what she could not bear. The voice destroyed the face, destroyed the man wholly. It was not rough and cordial like that of certain workmen, it was too soft for his vigorous body, it was weak and flabby.

"Be quiet," she said, "oh! be quiet. I want to try to talk to you, in spite of everything. . . ."

She stood looking at him, once more enslaved. He instinctively drew his hands from his head and sat up; she cowed him, perhaps.

"I don't know you," she continued, "but someone has talked to me about you."

Each word was an effort; all of a sudden, in a fit of giddiness, words, sentences, rushed from her lips with irresistible vehemence:

"Yes, someone has talked to me about you. Someone who is no longer here. I suppose you know whom I mean. He has written to me twice about you, two long letters, and the last one was horrifying. No one knows that I received it. He talked about you, indeed he did. I didn't know, I didn't understand what it was all about. If I could only have guessed I would never have consented to see you, but now it's too late. I've seen you and here you are, before my eyes. It was I who asked Arlette . . ."

She had a sudden feeling that she was losing the game by saying the last sentence, and, white with anxiety, bit her lips.

"What did you ask Arlette?" he demanded gloomily.

Now he looked at her with perfect self-possession and scarcely veiled contempt. Raising himself with one elbow, he sat up, then left his seat and went to the window, and she heard him whistling softly under his breath. He had drawn the curtain aside with one hand and watched the passers-by.

"I feel sorry for you," she said all of a sudden.

He let the curtain drop.

"What was that?" he asked, turning around.

"It's not your fault," she continued, standing very straight in the twilight. "It's your misfortune, a very great misfortune for you."

He burst out laughing, and Hedwige turned very red.

"It's the first time anyone has ever said that to me," he cried. "You can keep your pity, Mademoiselle. I'm not to be pitied." And furious, suddenly, he added: "So that's what Jean says in his letters, is it? Well, I could tell you a thing or two about him, you know! When you next write to him, you can tell him . . ."

He walked up to her. She stopped him with a single sentence:

"Jean is dead."

Gaston opened his mouth and was wordless for a few seconds.

"It's not true," he said at last.

For a short time, they faced each other, motionless. She saw his face against the light. The somewhat heavy jaw and powerful neck were outlined by a beam of light, and for the first time she had the impression of existing in his eyes because she knew something that he wanted to know and felt a glance full of curiosity weighing on her.

"You're just saying this to pull my leg," he said in his flaccid voice that slurred over the syllables.

"No," she replied. "He wrote first, and then we heard. He killed himself, he took poison in Naples, last week."

She said this almost in one breath, but she would have liked to prolong the sentence indefinitely, because he listened. Gaston had unconsciously come close to her and watched her with a frown, his eyes fixed and shining. She felt his warm breath on her flesh and did not move.

"Yes," she said in a kind of whisper, "poison, out of despair, and he talked about you in his last letter."

"Well, I never!" he muttered.

Hedwige thought that she would fall backwards and leaned against the table; the blood throbbed throughout her body, in her breast, her neck, her head. She opened her mouth; without making the slightest sound, she articulated his name, Gaston, but he did not notice the movement of lips that silently parted. Suddenly glancing at his wrist watch he said in an emotionless voice:

"You must excuse me. I'm late as it is."

He disappeared with a slight nod. She heard him tear down the stairs, then caught these words:

"Arlette! Hey, Arlette! Did you know that Jean had killed himself?"

After a great hubbub of exclamations, Gaston's voice was heard again:

"Couldn't that fool have sent me my money before dying? It's a damn shame. It was an understood thing. He had promised to let me have a thousand francs before the end of the month."

Hedwige sank into an armchair and stopped her ears with both hands.

Chapter 6

When she crossed the Vasseurs' threshold once more it was almost dark, and she could slip into the old house without being seen by anyone. Avoiding the great marble staircase and its lantern's glaring light, she walked down a passage that led to an older staircase whose wooden steps took her up to her bedroom, but it was so dark there that she ran into someone and a little frightened cry escaped her. It was the dressmaker, who apologized profusely:

"Mademoiselle didn't see me! I had a word to say to the housemaid. I don't know why Madame doesn't stand a lighted lamp on the table by the pantry door. . . ."

She talked faster than usual, and Hedwige drew away from her, a hand on the banister, filled with a sudden disgust that she could not understand at first.

"Isn't Mademoiselle dining?" asked the dressmaker. "They're all of them a little late this evening. If you could have heard the row that went on just now!"

She lowered her voice a little and continued:

"The cook told me all about it. They had just finished their soup. The door of the dumb-waiter was open and Berthe listened from the pantry."

She laughed, in the darkness, like a sly old child. Then it was that Hedwige realized that she smelt of spirits.

"That will do," she said. "Let me pass."

"Ah! So Mademoiselle is giving herself airs, like her cousin Ulrique," continued the dressmaker, leaning against the wall.

"I don't know what's come over you, Félicie," murmured Hedwige.

"What's come over me? Why, nothing at all. But Mademoiselle doesn't know. Just listen!"

She laid her hand on Hedwige's arm. The girl stood motionless; something prevented her from taking a step, from setting her foot on the first stair; she was obliged to stay there without moving, spellbound, and listen till the end to what this garrulous voice had to say. Her eyes grew accustomed to the darkness by degrees, and she distinguished the dressmaker's gray head and her narrow little shoulders outlined in black against the white wall. There was a short silence and the voice took up:

"In fact, it was about Monsieur Jean. His trunk was sent back from over there and Madame Vasseur opened it with Madame Pauque and Monsieur Raoul insisted on examining every single thing in it. They found letters. You can't imagine how Monsieur Raoul bellowed. He said it was a good thing that man was dead and that if he, Monsieur Raoul, had known about all this, he would have put him out of the house, because Monsieur Raoul won't have any trifling where morals are concerned, and it seems that Monsieur Jean borrowed a good many thousand-franc notes from him to give to Monsieur Dolange. . . ."

"No!" whispered Hedwige.

"Yes, he did. Gaston Dolange. It seems that he accepts money."

The voice grew lower, become almost unintelligible. In a kind of whisper that, after a strange fashion, resembled an old woman's prayers, Hedwige heard the following words that stood out from the rest:

". . . for money . . . with men . . . you understand . . ."

"I want you to go away," murmured Hedwige.

Her hand tightened on the stair rail; she walked up one step, with an effort.

"So it's no good your being set on him," continued the dressmaker. "It's too pitiful, Mademoiselle. You can imagine that everyone knows all about it, in the kitchen and elsewhere. . . ."

Hedwige walked slowly up the steps.

"Elsewhere too," repeated the dressmaker, whose whisper grew hoarser in an effort to be heard.

"Hold your tongue," begged Hedwige.

But the old maid continued from the bottom of the staircase:

"If it isn't too bad! A girl like you fretting her heart out over that! For nothing can be done about it, you know, nothing can be done. It's just as though they had a disease, so to speak."

Without answering, Hedwige walked up the few steps that separated her from her room and opened the door at once. The voice continued in the shadowy stairs:

"There's no lack of young men who could love you, Mademoiselle Hedwige. And I too could have been loved, if I hadn't had so many misfortunes. . . ."

Hedwige closed the door. The lamp she immediately turned on showed her bedroom in a soft pink light. Everything was tidy: the bedcover folded on an armchair and the sheet turned down at right angles. She walked to the window and opened it slightly. The night air laid a delicious freshness over her burning forehead and cheeks; for a moment she held her eyes shut the better to retain the shadow's diffused caress, when suddenly, as she remembered her visit to the antique dealer, her heart sank. For the last half-hour, there had been moments when she forgot, and then, suddenly, she recalled a word. Her memory became like a light that was extinguished and lit again continually, and each time Hedwige suffered so much that she wanted to die. At the bottom of her heart, she had always had a knowledge of a truth that frightened her; she had thought that she could destroy it merely by closing her eyes to it. Had not Ulrique once talked to her about these things?

She threw herself down on the bed, her face in the pillow as though someone had taken her by the shoulders and pressed her down, and a ridiculous voice said to her mentally: "You're creasing your dress." "Yes," she answered, panting, "I'm creasing it and I'm dying."

Some time went by, then she said out loud, in a hoarse voice, the sound of which astonished her: "He won't have me." Suddenly, in the darkness she made by shielding her face, she saw him. He looked at her with a displeased face and the bored expression that made her frantic, for she could imagine that same face transfigured with joy at the sight of other sights than that of an unhappy girl. Most distinctly, she saw his light blue eyes, whose pupils grew so large as to make them seem black, a mouth whose lips parted and glistened as though they were moist, and this face filled her with shame and inordinate longing, although she would not acknowledge it.

She got up suddenly and the vision disappeared. "There's no lack of young men who could love you. . . ." The dressmaker's words came back to her with cruel accuracy.

"Then why do I have to love a man like this one, who can't love me?" she murmured.

She had never put the question so clearly, and it gave her a shock, as though some great injustice had been suddenly revealed. In her eyes, for the last hour, her life was changing. She saw a succession of days beginning at her childhood and leading up to the unbearable minute she was enduring at present. She had been brought into the world in order that one evening, in a peaceful, banal little room, she should become conscious of a disaster beyond which nothing existed, for tomorrow was a meaningless word: she could not imagine what tomorrow could be for her, she could more easily imagine what tomorrow could be without her, as one pictures a house where one no longer lives.

"What's the matter with me?" she whispered.

At that moment, she heard the sound of a door opening on the ground floor and M. Vasseur's voice calling her. The dressmaker had probably told the servants that she had come home, and they had informed their masters. Her hands shook. She turned out the light instinctively and felt her way to the door. They were looking for her. She must hide and run away. Crossing the landing, she walked noiselessly down the passage, and M. Vasseur's voice reached her once more. He could not be very far, at the foot of the stairs, no doubt, but he could not know where she was. He would begin by looking for her in her room. She went straight ahead in the dark. She did not want to see anyone, she wanted to be alone, alone forever.

A carpet muffled her footsteps. She stole very softly to the end of the passage and stopped at the door of a room as M. Vasseur went up the stairs. Hedwige knew that he could neither see nor hear her if she kept perfectly still, but her heart beat faster, as though some terrible danger drew near. Leaning against the door, she thought that she heard a hum of voices inside the room, and the sound blending with M. Vasseur's footsteps was like an unknown tongue spoken softly, rapidly. Hedwige was frightened. Her uncle opened the door of her room and called her in the weary voice he had of evenings. She did not move. The sound that she thought she had heard stopped. It could only have been a delusion. With a sudden movement, she grasped the doorknob and entered. It was Raoul's room. She softly closed the door and turned on the electric light. The furniture became visible, with a sort of violence: the desk, the two stiff armchairs, the brass bed, the bedside table, and above the bed, the long tiresome photograph. Hedwige opened the drawer of the little table and took out the revolver.

"I'm going to kill him," she whispered.

But she turned the barrel of the little weapon against her own breast, and all of a sudden she cried out, and that great loud cry held all her ignorance of life, all her ignorance of herself. It was the cry of a child.

"How does it work?"

The shot went off. She stumbled and fell backward between one foot of the bed and the mahogany armchair. From the middle of the ceiling, an electric bulb watched her.